A LETTER TO MY LOVE

Devastated when Marcus married someone else, Sorrel resolved to devote her life to her toyshop and her invalid cousin, Alyse. However, when she meets Carl, the Bavarian woodcarver, it provides a romantic distraction — but Marcus's growing friendship with Alyse unsettles Sorrel. She is torn between her still-present love for Marcus, and her cousin's happiness. When Marcus's spiteful sister, Pamela, decides to repossess the toyshop for a wine bar, Sorrel decides to fight them both.

TONI ANDERS

◆

A LETTER
TO MY LOVE

Complete and Unabridged

LINFORD
Leicester

First published in Great Britain in 2006

First Linford Edition
published 2007

British Library CIP Data

Anders, Toni
    A letter to my love.—Large print ed.—
Linford romance library
    1. Love stories
    2. Large type books
    I. Title
    823.9'2 [F]

    ISBN 978–1–84617–942–6

Published by
F. A. Thorpe (Publishing)
Anstey, Leicestershire

Set by Words & Graphics Ltd.
Anstey, Leicestershire
Printed and bound in Great Britain by
T. J. International Ltd., Padstow, Cornwall

This book is printed on acid-free paper

'Forget Him...'

Sorrel leaned into the back of the shop window and carefully placed a small boy doll on a swing in the garden of the doll's house, then studied the effect with pleasure. The red-roofed dolls' house and its occupants had arrived that morning from the manufacturers and she had been longing all day for time to arrange them in the centre of the window.

Now, at five o'clock, and with the 'CLOSED' sign on the door, she could concentrate on her new stock.

She unfastened a large box, took out six dolls in party dresses and placed them on little chairs in one corner of the window. In the opposite corner, large brightly-coloured balls surrounded a gleaming green tricycle.

That left a large space in the middle for old Ernst's toys, the speciality of her

1

shop. Beautifully carved and brightly painted, they were popular with the locals and visitors alike. Sorrel liked to think how many Christmas stockings and birthday parties they had graced.

She placed a selection in front of the dolls' house: pull-along yellow ducks; steam trains with carriages; wooden animals; clowns and trolleys full of coloured bricks.

With her head on one side, she studied the window with satisfaction. Her long brown hair swung across her face and she tucked it back behind her ear. She usually wore it tied back but it was good to feel it free when the shop was closed.

'Cup of tea?' called Alyse from the kitchen behind the shop.

'Please. Just pour it out — I shan't be a moment. I want to go outside and look at my new window display.'

On the pavement, she looked at the window critically but could see no faults. She glanced up at the sign above the window. The Toybox. Excitement tingled through her body every time she saw it. Her own toyshop! Dreamed of since childhood and now a reality for three years. Smiling to herself, she moved towards the door and the welcome cup of tea.

Horses hooves clattered behind her on the cobbled road and two riders appeared around the corner.

The girl in front was immaculately turned out in smooth-fitting jodhpurs and black riding jacket. Her hair was tied back beneath her hard hat, but a glimpse of auburn could be seen. She gave Sorrel the slightest acknowledgement by a nod of her head and rode on.

The man on the horse behind was more casually dressed, but wore his boots, jeans and dark green sweater with a certain air. He sat confidently in the saddle and as he came level with Sorrel he reined in his mount.

'Good afternoon, Sorrel.' He gave a slight bow. 'I haven't seen you for some time. I hope you're well.'

'Very well, thank you, Marcus.' What

a ridiculously stilted conversation, she thought, unable to form her features into a smile.

'New stock?' He gestured towards the window with his riding crop.

'Yes. I'm doing a different display.'

'It's very colourful, very eye-catching.'

Sorrel said nothing.

He gave her a long look from his deep grey eyes, then a farewell salute with his hand. In a few moments, horse and rider had disappeared down the road.

Sorrel went into the shop. Pleasure in her new window had gone.

'Drat those Barringtons,' she muttered, checking the door and setting the alarm. 'Arrogant — stuck up . . . ' She was still muttering as she entered the cosy little living-room.

Alyse, her cousin, was sitting at a small round table in front of the fire. She glanced up as Sorrel entered. 'You look like you're in a bad mood. Don't you like the new dolls' house?'

Sorrel sank into the opposite chair.

'The dolls' house is fine. And I'm pleased with the new window, it looks good.'

'So why the face like thunder?'

Alyse handed her a cup of tea and pushed a plate of small iced cakes towards her. Sorrel sipped the tea, selected a cake and sank back into the soft armchair cushions.

'Marcus and Pamela Barrington,' she said. 'You don't know them but Marcus is my landlord. He owns my shop. In fact, he owns half of St Towan.'

Alyse pulled herself awkwardly out of her chair and went to a drawer for her manicure set. Returning, she lowered herself with a little grimace.

'Is it bad today?' Sorrel asked sympathetically.

'I'll live.' Alyse busied herself with a broken nail. 'What's wrong with Marcus?' she asked, not looking at her cousin.

'If you have nothing to do all night, I can explain. Otherwise — ' scowling, Sorrel took another cake ' — it would take too long. Looking down at me in that lordly way. He's done nothing for his money — inherited it, not worked for it.'

'If he was on a horse, he would have to look down at you,' Alyse pointed out reasonably.

'Don't stick up for him! You don't know the man, you've only lived here a few months. Wait till you meet him, then you'll find out how insufferable he is.'

'Actually,' Alyse fastened the manicure set, 'I have met him. And he was very helpful.'

Sorrel sat up. 'You've met him? Where?'

'In the library, two or three weeks ago. I had a small fine on a book — you know, the one on the history of Cornwall. I kept it too long.'

'Yes, I remember.' Sorrel's voice was impatient. 'But where does Marcus come in?'

'Well, I had no change — just a ten-pound note — and neither did the assistant. I had just decided to wait until the next time I went in, when the man behind me put a handful of change on the counter. So everything was sorted out. He had a lovely smile,' she added, 'and deep grey eyes.'

'How do you know it was Marcus Barrington?'

'When he'd gone, the assistant asked me if I knew who he was. She told me it was Marcus. She giggled a bit and said, 'Isn't he gorgeous? And he's not married!' So if he's not married, who's Pamela?'

'His sister. She has red hair and a temper to match.'

'You *are* in a mood! Does he always have this effect on you?'

Sorrel stood up. 'I'm sorry, Alyse, don't mind me. I've been busy today and I'm quite tired. Do you want any help with dinner?'

'It's only roast chicken and salad,' said Alyse. 'It'll be ready when you are. Why don't you have a warm bubbly bath and relax?'

'Good idea. Thanks, Al. But just a final word on the subject — be careful. Don't get carried away by a smile and a pair of deep grey eyes.'

'No, Grandma,' said Alyse demurely.

Sorrel threw a cushion at her and went upstairs, humming, her cheerful mood restored. It had been a good move to ask Alyse to live with her. Now, after a busy day in the shop, there was a tasty dinner waiting for her each evening instead of a scratch meal on the corner of the kitchen table.

Not that the luck was all on her side. Alyse now had a comfortable home and someone near her all the time. The problem was her hip, which had prevented her from working any longer, and also made it hard for her to live alone.

Sorrel's offer of a home with her in the little Cornish town of St Towan had seemed like a miracle. She was younger than Sorrel and they had grown up miles apart, but they now shared the house happily enough.

Alyse had days when the pain made it necessary to rest for hours, but she could usually manage light housework and could cope with shopping in the less hilly part of the town.

In the bathroom, Sorrel felt herself relax as she breathed in the luxurious scent of the vanilla bath oil Alyse had given her for her birthday and watched the bubbles rise higher and higher up the bath.

She lit two fat cream vanilla candles and switched off the overhead light, then lowered herself into the silky water. Marcus Barrington. What do I care for Marcus Barrington? He's in the past. Forget him. She forced her mind to become blank, lay back against her bath pillow and closed her eyes.

★   ★   ★

Their sitting-room was upstairs above the shop, a pretty room decorated in shades of aquamarine to reflect the colours of the summer sea. There was a small, closed balcony overlooking the sea, which Sorrel had furnished with chairs and a small table, and she loved to sit there and enjoy the changing moods of the water, from soft, rippling billows to wild rampaging waves.

Whatever the season, there was something interesting to see.

The sandy beaches with their trippers and noise were farther round the headland. The beach opposite the toy shop was rocky and strewn with boulders and usually deserted.

Sometimes the rocks were covered with huge grey and white seagulls, screeching and calling to each other in what Sorrel thought of as wild, maniacal laughs.

On the rocks in front of the caves below the headland she would sometimes see the soft faces and huge, melancholy eyes of grey seals, often with their babies.

If Alyse didn't want to climb the stairs, Sorrel would sit alone after dinner gazing out across the water. She felt unkind admitting it, even to herself, but actually she preferred to be there alone, idly thinking over the events of the day, until, as often happened, Marcus Barrington intruded into her thoughts. Then she would sigh and go downstairs to her cousin. Alyse's fair, curly head was usually bent over her embroidery as she listened to a story tape.

This evening, as Sorrel came into the room, Alyse reached for the pause button, but Sorrel lifted a hand in protest.

'No, don't disturb yourself. I'm going out. What are you listening to tonight?'

'Gone With The Wind. I've played it so often, I know it by heart. I love stories set in America. I should like to live there. Would you?'

Sorrel shook her head. 'I can't imagine living anywhere but here.'

'But if you fell in love, you'd live where he lived surely?'

'I could never live anywhere but Cornwall,' Sorrel said decisively. 'You're just a romantic, you are!'

'I think you are, too, deep down,' Alyse countered. 'You just pretend to be a hard-nosed businesswoman. Inside, you're waiting for a handsome prince to sweep you off your feet!'

Sorrel gave her an exasperated look. 'I really don't think so! Anyway, I shan't be long.' She put on her cream knitted jacket. 'Just in case. It's a beautiful evening but it may be cold later on.'

'Are you going for a walk? Would you like me to come with you?' Alyse offered even though walking could be painful for her.

Sorrel smiled and shook her head. 'Thanks, but I'm going up to see Ernst. He wasn't too well when I saw him at the weekend. But you know him, never complains.'

'Give him my best wishes.' Alyse settled back comfortably in her chair, picked up her embroidery and switched on her story tape again.

★ ★ ★

It was a beautiful evening with the slight coolness of early Autumn. Sorrel paused for a while, leaning on the sea wall, breathing in the pungent smell of seaweed on the rocks below and watching a little motor-boat buzzing up and down the bay. Then she resumed her walk, climbing the hill towards the headland.

Halfway up, a row of small colour-washed cottages balanced precariously almost on the edge of the cliff. Once they had been the homes of fishermen, often housing large families of children. Now, some were holiday cottages, a few others the homes of artists. The last one was occupied by Ernst Schumann, the old toy maker.

Ernst had appeared in her shop soon after she'd opened three years ago, and they had been friends ever since. The fifty years difference in their ages seemed not to exist. Before the arrival of Alyse, Sorrel had spent many of her evenings in Ernst's workshop watching as the old man carved and planed pieces of wood to eventually reveal a magical toy which he painted in glowing colours.

He'd taught her how to use tools safely, how to select the right piece of wood and occasionally allowed her to paint a simple object.

Sometimes Ernst walked down the hill to her shop to show her his latest creation. He loved to sit in the corner of the shop for an hour or so watching children playing with his toys and chatting to their parents.

Occasionally Alyse persuaded him to stay for a meal. He never spoke of his family and Sorrel wouldn't pry. She knew by his name and accent that he came from Germany, but that was all.

However, it was a few weeks now since Ernst had produced a new toy, and he seemed to be getting more and more frail. Sorrel was worried about him.

As she reached his gate, Mrs Tregarron, his next-door neighbour, came out of her house and waved.

'He's not at all well,' she said. 'I tried to give him some soup this morning but he said he wasn't hungry. But he won't let me send for the doctor.'

Sorrel thanked her for her concern. 'I'll see what I can do,' she said.

She tapped on the door. Shuffling sounds could be heard from inside the cottage, then the door was hesitantly opened and Ernst peeped out, a thick blanket wrapped around his shoulders. The cottage was warm but he seemed to be shivering.

Sorrel put an arm about him and guided him to the rocking-chair by the fire. He smiled up at her lovingly. 'It is so good to see you, *liebchen*.'

'What have you eaten today?' she asked gently.

The old man shrugged. 'Perhaps a little bread and butter this morning. I don't remember.'

'Could you eat an omelette?' the girl asked.

Ernst looked doubtful.

'An omelette would be very light,' she

pressed. 'It would do you good.'

He took her hand between his two gnarled ones. 'You are very kind, *liebchen*.'

In the neat little kitchen, Sorrel made tea and an omelette and cut thin slices of bread and butter. She carried the tray through to the sitting-room and was cheered by the pleasure on his face as he began to eat.

'You haven't been down to see me for two weeks,' she chided.

'I have been tired,' he said simply.

'So no new toys?'

The toy maker's old eyes lit up. '*Ja*, one new toy. It is on the bench in the workshop.'

Sorrel went through to the little workshop with its smell of wood chippings and glue. The tools were neatly arranged on a bench at the back of the room or hung in rows from hooks on the walls. The floor had been swept and everything was clean and neat. In the middle of the centre bench stood the new toy.

'Oh-h-h.' She lifted the gleaming enamelled parrot and studied the perfection of its feathers and claws and curved beak. It was exquisite.

She carried the bird and its stand into the sitting-room and put it on the table. When set in motion, the parrot rocked to and fro on the perch as if it would never stop.

Ernst smiled proudly. 'One of my best models, I think.'

'It's beautiful. What do you say — *schön*? How many have you finished?' She was anxious to have them for her new display.

'That is the only one,' he said quietly. 'I am so tired.

Fear swept over her as she studied her old friend. 'I'm going to call the doctor,' she said.

'*Nein*. No, please. No doctor. I shall go to bed and rest. I shall soon be well.'

'But why can't I call the doctor?'

'He will send me to the hospital. I don't want to leave my home.'

Sorrel looked at him in despair. 'Well,

if you won't let me call the doctor, I'm going to fill some hot-water bottles and make sure you go to bed now.'

He didn't protest and she set about her task.

'I shall be back first thing in the morning,' she said when she had settled him into bed. 'Alyse can open the shop for me. She sends you her best wishes, by the way.'

The old man smiled faintly. 'She is very kind, the little Alyse.'

'And if you're no better, I shall call the doctor whatever you say.' She made a mock cross face at him and left the bedroom.

She tidied the sitting-room and let herself out of the cottage.

It was a fine evening with just a light warm breeze. She decided not to go straight home but to stretch her legs with a walk to the headland.

She set off slowly up the steep hill, still thinking of Ernst. She had never really considered that he must be old and that one day he would be unable to carve the beautiful toys she loved to sell. If he had to retire, where would she find another toy maker? She would have to give the matter some thought.

There were a few people on the cliff top, walking to and fro, or sprawling on the soft turf. The sun had sunk low on the horizon leaving a golden path of light across the sea towards them. Everyone seemed reluctant to leave such a lovely evening.

Most of the people were in couples and she wished for a moment that *she* had someone special, someone with whom to share a gentle stroll. But there had been no-one since . . . Forget him, she told herself furiously. Why did her thoughts keep coming back to him? It was years ago . . .

'Sorrel, hi! What are you doing here all on your own?' The speaker had been lounging on the springy turf with a group of five or six young men, but now jumped to his feet, a large teddy-bear of a man with dark golden hair and a short golden beard.

'Exercise,' she said shortly.

Tony Redvers was an old school friend. They went out occasionally but there was no romantic interest — not on Sorrel's part, anyway. Tony took her out hoping that one day she would see him as the love of her life, but he knew it was unlikely.

'Come for a drink?' he invited.

'Your friends . . . ' She glanced at the group of young men.

'Don't worry about them, they won't even notice I've gone. We'll go to the Schooner.'

'Just one drink then. I told Alyse I wouldn't be long.'

'She won't mind. I'll bet she's lost in one of her story tapes.'

Sorrel laughed. 'How did you guess? She loves them. Hardly ever watches television. I don't think she can watch television and do her embroidery.'

They walked down the hill, turned left at the bottom and soon reached the Schooner Inn.

Tony gestured towards the garden.

'D'you want to sit outside?'

'It's getting a bit chilly now. Let's see if there's any room inside.'

The lounge was bright and full of noise and laughter. Sorrel found a table while Tony went to the bar.

After a few minutes, she was surprised to find herself enjoying the atmosphere. Her visit to Ernst had made her feel quite depressed. Poor Ernst. She hoped he was sleeping soundly; it would help him to recover.

Tony came back with their drinks.

'I was watching you just now,' he said. 'You looked quite sad. Is anything wrong?'

She told him about Ernst.

'Poor old thing,' he commiserated. 'And he has no family to look after him, has he?'

'I don't know anything about him. He's a strange person to find in a Cornish town — a German toy maker. I wonder how he came to be here?'

'Actually I know about that,' said Tony. 'He was a prisoner of war. Stayed on after his comrades went back to Germany. Married a Cornish girl, but the marriage didn't last.'

'How do you know all this?'

'My parents were talking about him one evening. They know Mrs Tregarron, his next-door neighbour.' He emptied his glass. 'Another?'

'No thanks. I must get back.'

Tony helped her on with her jacket, holding her briefly against him as he did. She smiled and they pushed their way through the crowd.

In the doorway, a man about to enter stood back to let them pass. Tony was in front and stepped on to the pavement, but as Sorrel went to pass the man caught her arm. It was Marcus Barrington.

'Sorrel, I must talk to you.'

She looked pointedly at the hand holding her arm and he removed it.

'I'm sorry, but can we talk? Can we meet some time — dinner perhaps?'

'I don't think we have anything to say to each other,' she returned coolly.

'I wish we could be friends. Can't we forget the past? When I saw you the other day . . . '

'I think that would be too difficult. So much has happened,' she said coldly. 'Goodnight, Marcus.'

Tony looked at her curiously as they walked towards her shop. 'Are you still friendly with Marcus Barrington? I'm surprised.'

'Don't be. I'm not still friendly with him. Here we are — are you coming in? Alyse would like to see you.'

'Not tonight thanks, but give her my best wishes. I'll be in touch.' He bent and gave her a light kiss and went off whistling softly to himself.

Sorrel watched him go. He was the best sort of friend, she decided; uncomplicated, accepting what she was willing to give.

★ ★ ★

Alyse was making a cup of tea when she got in. She smiled as Sorrel entered.

23

'Would you like a sandwich? There's plenty of chicken left.'

'Nothing for me, thanks. I've been to the Schooner with Tony Redvers and I'm full of spritzer.'

'How was Ernst?'

Sorrel told her and Alyse looked concerned. 'Will he be all right?'

'I think so. He looked quite comfortable when I left him. I'll go up and see him first thing if you'll open the shop for me.'

As she prepared for bed, Sorrel thought of her confrontation with Marcus. Why hadn't she mentioned it to Alyse? She supposed it was because Alyse would then need to know the whole story. And if her cousin had decided that she wanted to know Marcus better, why should Sorrel interfere? Alyse had few friends in St Towan.

A sudden thought struck her. Marcus had said he wanted to talk to her. Perhaps it was something to do with Alyse. Perhaps his efforts to get back into her own good books was because he had fallen for Alyse. Love at first sight. It happened.

But this would put a new slant on her relationship with her cousin. She loved Alyse. She had no feeling for Marcus, had she? Had she? Could she accept their friendship calmly? Would it matter to her? Would it ever happen?

Well, time would tell. In a small place like St Towan, it wouldn't be long before she would see Marcus again and it would become clear which cousin held his interest.

She climbed into bed and opened a book, but after reading the same paragraph six times, she closed it and lay back, thinking. *Had* Alyse met Marcus only once — in the library? She had talked as if she knew him rather better than that.

It was no use. She couldn't sleep with it on her mind. She got out of bed, put on her dressing-gown and went downstairs. There was a light under her cousin's bedroom door. Sorrel turned the handle. Alyse was sitting up in bed reading. She looked up, startled, as Sorrel came in.

'Is anything wrong?'

'I'm sorry, Al — there's something on my mind. I know it's silly but — you said you met Marcus Barrington in the library. Is that the only time you've seen him?'

She looked dumbfounded by such an odd question at this time of night, but answered easily.

'I've bumped into him in town and we've met for a coffee a few times. Does it matter?'

Sorrel looked at her but said nothing.

'I suppose I might have mentioned it but it was no big deal,' Alyse added. 'And you were so tied up with the shop. Anyway, a few days later I met him in the library, I was in the café overlooking the harbour when Marcus came in. I recognised him at once, but I didn't think he'd recognise me.'

'But he did?'

'Yes. He came over and asked if he

could join me. I expect it was because I had the best table, right by the window.' She giggled. 'I was ready to go but he bought me another coffee and we chatted for ages — at least an hour.'

'Good gracious! What about?' What could Marcus and Alyse possibly have in common, Sorrel wondered.

'Oh, all sorts of things,' Alyse returned artlessly. 'He's easy to talk to, isn't he?'

'And you saw him again?'

'Yes. A week later. We arranged to meet in the same place.'

'You'll get yourself talked about, making assignations with the town's most eligible bachelor!' Sorrel tried to make a joke of it, but there was a telling edge to her voice.

'I told him about my hip that time, and about the surgeon in America who's operating on people like me with amazing results. I told him I'm saving up to go to America.'

'What did he say?' Sorrel asked.

'He didn't say much. I expect he

thinks I'm silly hoping to save that sort of money. After all, I don't even have a proper job!' She blinked a few times and there was the suspicion of tears on her lashes.

Back in her bedroom, Sorrel climbed into bed and switched off the light. If only I could give Alyse the money, she thought. But a toyshop in a small town would never be a gold-mine. She and Alyse lived comfortably enough, but expensive operations in America weren't on the agenda.

She closed her eyes. Better get some sleep if she had to get up early to visit old Ernst.

Two Precious Gifts

Sorrel woke early the next morning with the feeling that something was wrong. For a few moments she lay still, listening to the harsh calls of the seagulls and the splash of water on rocks. Still half asleep, she felt uneasy. But what was wrong?

Then she remembered. Ernst. Her eyes shot open and she was suddenly wide awake. She had to go and see Ernst.

Shivering in the chill of the autumn morning, she wrapped herself in her warm dressing-gown, slipped her feet into her slippers and made her way downstairs. Everything was quiet. Alyse was still asleep, deep under her duvet.

Ten minutes later, Sorrel carried a tray of tea into her cousin's bedroom.

Alyse reached sleepily for her bedside clock. 'What time is it? Have I overslept?'

'No. I'm sorry to wake you early but I want to go and see Ernst. I have an awful feeling that something has happened. I'll go round as soon as I'm dressed, I won't wait for breakfast.'

Alyse knew better than to argue with her. She sipped her tea.

'Don't worry about the shop, I'll see to everything.'

'Bless you.' Sorrel smiled gratefully. 'Now I'll go and dress.'

Half an hour later, she was hurrying up the hill, glad that the exercise would warm her up. The sea lay flat and grey, scarcely moving. How depressing everything looked when there was no sunshine. Grey sea, grey rocks and grey granite houses.

She knocked softly on the front door of the old man's cottage. There was no answer. She had a key, for use in an emergency. Well, this seemed to be an emergency. Fearfully she inserted it into the lock.

Mrs Tregarron opened her front

door. 'There you are, Miss Basset. I've been looking out for you. I knew you'd be up this morning.'

'How is he?' Sorrel's voice was anxious.

'Gone to hospital. In the middle of the night.' Mrs Tregarron's face was alight with the drama of her news.

'In the middle of the night? But . . . '

'We heard noises at about two o'clock. Didn't know what it was, of course, but we were worried. So, Albert — that's my husband — went round to see if there was a problem. We've got a key, you see, just in case.'

'And . . . ?'

'Old Ernst was on the floor. He'd got out of bed and fallen down. So we phoned for an ambulance and they took him to hospital. We just had time to gather a few bits and pieces together for him.'

Sorrel hurried back down the hill. Please let Alyse be well enough to look after the shop this morning, she prayed, then I can go and see Ernst.

Alyse was bright and cheerful. 'Toast?' she asked as Sorrel hurried in and flung her coat on the chair. 'I'm just making some before I open the shop. Is Ernst any better this morning?'

Hot buttered toast was comforting. Sorrel ate three pieces while she told Alyse about Ernst.

'I'd like to go and see him at the hospital as soon as possible, if you think you can cope here.'

'Of course. I feel fine — no pain at all today.'

'Well, if you're sure . . . And you must rest all afternoon.'

★ ★ ★

Parking spaces were a rarity in St Towan. The twisting streets and alleys had been built long before the days of the car, and Sorrel had to climb the steep main street of the town to reach the carpark at the top where she kept her own small car.

On the way, she went into several

shops to amass a small collection of goodies for Ernst — chocolate, a packet of the little sponge cakes she knew he liked, and a book of photographs of Cornwall. She couldn't imagine him reading a novel, but perhaps pictures of the place he loved so much would cheer him up.

At the hospital she explained who she was and begged special permission to see him although it wasn't visiting hours. His eyes were closed and but for the slight twitching of the blue-veined hands on the coverlet, there was no indication of life.

Quietly she pulled a chair near to the bed and put one hand over his. He opened his eyes.

'*Liebchen*, you've come to see me.'

'Oh, Ernst.' Her eyes filled with tears. 'I had such a shock when I got to your cottage this morning.'

He grimaced. 'It happened in the night. I fell.'

'Mrs Tregarron told me. Don't worry about it. You're in the best place now.

I'm sure you'll soon be well and able to go home.'

'Home.' The word was a quiet sigh on his lips. He closed his eyes. 'Home,' he said again, then lay so quiet that Sorrel thought he had fallen asleep.

The daily routine of the ward went on around them. A nurse checked a drip on the patient in the next bed. Opposite, screens were pulled into place and an important-looking man in a white coat, followed by a flock of younger ones, disappeared behind them.

Through all the commotion, Ernst lay unmoving. Sorrel was unsure whether he was asleep, but he seemed so peaceful she was afraid to move and disturb him.

Then his lids flickered and he opened his eyes. 'My home was in Bavaria. Have you been to Bavaria, *liebchen*?'

'No.' Her voice was soft. 'Tell me about it.'

'Trees,' he said. 'Trees everywhere, with little paths in and out.' He waved his hand feebly. 'So dark and mysterious and peaceful.' He was quiet again. Sorrel waited.

'And castles.' His face creased into a little smile. 'Castles. So beautiful. Like a fairy tale. Neuschwanstein, that is the most magical. You must see Neuschwanstein.'

'I've seen photographs,' said Sorrel. 'Pointed towers rising up high above the trees. Walt Disney copied it.'

'And in the snow, it glistens.' He seemed not to hear her. He was far away. 'So beautiful,' he repeated softly. 'You must go and see it one day. Promise you will go — for me.'

She pressed her hand over his again. 'I promise.'

A nurse appeared at the bedside. 'Mr Schumann must rest now,' she said.

Sorrel stood up. 'Of course. May I telephone later to see how he is? I don't think he has any relatives in this country.'

'He gave us the name of a nephew in Germany. We've sent for him.' The nurse began to straighten the bedclothes and smooth the pillows. 'Telephone about five o'clock.'

Dismissed, Sorrel glanced back at her old friend and walked away, but almost immediately the nurse hurried after her. 'He has something for you. Can you come back for a moment?'

As Sorrel approached the bed, Ernst held out something towards her. She took it and found she was holding a tiny swan carved from soft golden wood. The detail was exquisite, each feather lifted and curling, the neck a graceful bend topped by a perfect head and the base carved into curling waves.

'The castle of Hohenschwangau. The swan is the symbol. I have had it all my life. Now I want you to have it.'

'Oh, Ernst. It's perfect! Did you carve it?'

'No. My father made it for my mother when they were sweethearts.'

'I'll treasure it always.' She bent and kissed the old man's brow. 'Rest now. I'll come again tomorrow.'

She left the ward clutching the swan, unable to see clearly for the tears filling her eyes.

When she got back to the shop, Alyse greeted her with what seemed an embarrassed laugh.

'Sorrel! I didn't expect you back so soon.'

'They wouldn't let me stay any longer. And I didn't want to leave you alone for too long.'

'I was quite all right,' Alyse protested. 'There have only been two customers. Why didn't you do some shopping or go for a coffee? You don't go into town very often.'

Sorrel studied her cousin. 'What's the matter, Alyse? You don't seem very pleased to see me.'

Just then the door opened and Marcus Barrington walked in, a plastic bag containing a loaf of bread swinging from his hand. He stopped when he saw Sorrel. Alyse coloured up.

'Marcus called in earlier and offered to get me a loaf,' she explained hastily.

'You know how much toast we ate this morning. Well, we were out of bread and . . . '

'Don't babble, Alyse.' Sorrel's tone was unusually sharp. 'I don't mind if Marcus wants to do the shopping for you.'

It was laughable. The grand Marcus Barrington shopping for bread. But she didn't feel like laughing. She was too worried about Ernst and she had been looking forward to a quiet lunch with Alyse. She turned to leave the room.

'Sorrel.' Marcus called her back. 'Would you mind if I took Alyse to lunch?'

She stopped but didn't turn round. 'Why should I mind? It's up to Alyse.'

'You could join us,' he suggested. 'Alyse told me about old Ernst. It would cheer you up to go out.'

'No, thank you, Marcus. I'd rather be alone.'

Alyse slipped past her. 'I'll just go and change then.'

Sorrel could hardly leave Marcus

alone in the shop with only a bag of bread for company. Resentfully she took it from him and led the way into the kitchen.

Undecided, she wondered how to broach the subject that was worrying her. Perhaps it would be best to come right out with it.

'Marcus, you do realise that Alyse isn't well?'

'Her hip? Yes, I know about that.'

'She's had a great deal of pain, and she's not strong. That's why I asked her to live with me. I hope you're not just — toying with her.' The words came out in a rush. 'She's had a lot to cope with in her life. I don't want her to be just — another notch on your gun.'

'Notch on my gun! What an expression! No, I'm not just toying with her. I've become very fond of Alyse. She's a sweet girl.'

'I don't want her to be hurt,' she insisted.

'I shan't hurt her. We're friends, nothing more.' He put a hand on her arm. 'Sorrel, you look so upset. You're not just bothered about Alyse, are you? Is Ernst really ill?'

'He's very weak.' Her voice was unsteady. 'I'm afraid he won't recover.'

'Are you very close to him?'

'Like you and Alyse,' she gave a wan smile, 'we're friends. Perhaps it seems strange but we hit it off straight away when we first met three years ago. We never talked about personal things, just toys. But he was such a gentle old man, I just relaxed when I was with him. And I know he liked to be with me. If he . . . if he . . . ' She couldn't go on.

'Come out to lunch with Alyse and me,' he urged. 'It'll take your mind off things. You can manage it, it's early closing today, isn't it?'

He was still holding her arm. They stood close together, so close that she could feel his breath on her cheek. For one wild moment she wanted his arms around her, holding her, comforting her . . .

She broke away and went to stand on

40

the opposite side of the room. After all this time, he still had the power to affect her, but she mustn't weaken.

'I'd love to show you what I've been doing to the estate,' he said. 'Prove to you that I'm not a playboy. Please come, Sorrel.'

Alyse came back into the room.

'Sorrel's coming, too,' Marcus told her.

Alyse smiled at her, looking genuinely pleased. 'Oh, good. I'm glad you've changed your mind.'

Have I? thought Sorrel. Or has it been changed for me? Marcus always did like to have his own way.

★　★　★

They drove two miles beyond St Towan, along the coast road. A signpost directed them to Pencarrock Barns and the car turned off the road, under a rough stone archway and over bumpy ground to the far corner of the car park.

'Sorry about the bumps, we haven't

got round to doing the car park yet,' Marcus apologised. 'There's not far to walk,' he assured Alyse as he helped her out of the back seat.

The air was fresh with the sharp tang of the sea. Two fields away, they could see the edge of sandhills and the greeny-blue of the sea.

Marcus took Alyse's arm and they made their way beneath another stone archway into a cobbled area surrounded by converted barns and farm outbuildings.

'It's like a little town,' Alyse commented. 'Are these shops?'

'They call them workshops and retail outlets but yes, they are shops. We'll have a look around when we've had some lunch. The restaurant is just round this corner.'

There were quite a few people wandering in and out of the shops, most carrying brightly-coloured carrier bags labelled 'Pencarrock Barns'. The restaurant was quiet.

'The rush is over,' Marcus explained,

settling them at a table. 'Most people seem to come early.'

The girls looked around with interest. Chairs and tables in pale wood gave the place a Scandinavian look. Blue linen curtains and place mats made a comfortable contrast and warm copperware glinted on shelves and wall brackets.

'It glows like honey,' said Alyse, and Marcus looked pleased.

A tall, elegant woman in blue came over with menus for them, and Sorrel was astonished to see that it was Pamela Barrington. The surprise must have shown on her face.

'Pamela manages the restaurant,' Marcus explained, and introduced her to Alyse.

Pamela looked surprised to see Sorrel with her brother, but made no comment as Marcus gave her murmured instructions, and soon they were sipping glasses of wine and studying the menu.

The meal was surprisingly good.

Sorrel had felt that a place that catered for day-trippers wouldn't have very ambitious standards, but she was pleasantly surprised, something that Marcus must have sensed.

'Pamela demands first class work from her staff,' he said, 'especially her chef. Now, if you've finished, shall we take a look round?'

The shops were interesting and varied. Each had bright lighting and the warm smell of new wood.

The girls exclaimed as they examined silk scarves in beautiful jewel colours; scented pot pourri in hand-thrown pottery bowls; rings and necklaces of semi-precious stones and exquisite filigree work.

In the Chocolate Boutique, a warm cave of deep, delicious smells, they sampled hand-made chocolates topped with crystallised violets and sugar-coated fruit. Marcus smiled at their enthusiasm and presented them with a round box of chocolates tied with a huge yellow bow.

Sorrel, who loved Christmas, bought a selection of unusual tree ornaments in the Christmas shop. Some were of brightly-painted wood and reminded her of Ernst, and for a moment she was sad.

Marcus noticed and, guessing the reason, hurried them on to a workshop where molten glass was being fashioned into little animals.

'Choose one,' he urged them. 'A memento of this afternoon.'

Alyse chose a kitten, while, without thinking, Sorrel picked up a swan. Marcus paid and they left the oppressive heat of the workshop.

By now, Alyse was beginning to tire, so Marcus led them to a small café where he ordered tea and cakes.

'Would you mind if we left you to rest for ten minutes?' he asked Alyse. 'I want to show Sorrel something else and I think you're really too tired to walk much farther. But we'll be very quick, I promise.'

He took Sorrel outside, across the

cobbled yard and pointed in the direction of the coast.

'Quite a few of them are deliberately obscured by trees,' he said, 'but I think you can see what they are.

'Houses?' she queried. 'No, they're too small. Chalets?'

'Exactly. Chalets for holiday visitors. I'm building a little chalet park. It'll be very quiet — no shops or clubs, just sea views and peace for people who love this coastline.'

'What a good idea. This part of the coast is so popular.'

They moved to another part of the barn complex. Again he pointed. 'And over there?'

'It's a golf course, isn't it?'

'It is. Almost finished. Again, mostly for visitors, but there are plenty of residents in the area who like golf and there isn't another course near here.'

'So this is what you've been doing since . . . since . . .'

'I've been working hard for the past two years since my father died. Perhaps

46

now you'll agree that I'm not just a playboy as you so obviously thought.' The idea seemed to rankle with him.

Sorrel looked away from him to the golf course. To say she was amazed was no exaggeration. That Marcus could be capable of such imagination and hard work had never crossed her mind.

'A shopping complex, a chalet park and a golf course,' she listed. 'You've certainly changed the Pencarrock Estate. What would your father have said?'

They looked towards the large granite house half a mile away, Pencarrock House, Marcus's family home.

'He would have approved — eventually. I'm going to make the place pay and I'm going to do it by myself. There's no future in his sort of farming nowadays.' His handsome face glowed with enthusiasm.

Oh, Marcus, she thought, why didn't you make these plans years ago? I would have helped you. Now it's too late. Alyse will love you but she can't work with you.

Sorrel felt guilty as they entered the café and saw Alyse's wan little face, and decided not to wait for a cup of tea but to get her cousin home as soon as possible. She and Marcus walked on either side of Alyse, supporting her on the short distance to the car.

'I'm so sorry to be a nuisance,' Alyse kept repeating, despite their protests. 'I've enjoyed this trip so much; it's just that my wretched hip hates to walk.' She tried to laugh but the pain made it difficult.

Marcus looked at Sorrel across the fair, curly head between them. *His* expression was hard to fathom.

They made Alyse comfortable in the back of the car with cushions to support her, and she did her best not to cry out when they hit a pothole or a bump. When they reached the toyshop, Marcus jumped out and lifted Alyse from the car to carry her inside.

Sorrel followed, her emotions in

turmoil. The sight of Alyse cradled in Marcus's arms, her fair head resting on his shoulder, made her realise the complications of the situation. Marcus could deny any love for Alyse but his tender demeanour contradicted his words.

Sorrel brushed away his offer of further help, thanked him for the afternoon and closed the door behind him with a sigh of relief.

'It's bed for you,' she told Alyse. 'No embroidery tonight. I'll help you into bed then I'll bring you up a bite of supper on a tray. What would you like?'

Alyse fancied nothing more than a bowl of soup. That was easily prepared and Sorrel relaxed in an armchair while her cousin drank the soup and ate a small bread roll.

'You look better already,' Sorrel commented.

'I was needing to rest.' Alyse smiled. 'But I did enjoy the afternoon.' She fingered the little glass kitten. 'Wasn't Marcus kind?'

'It was a very . . . interesting . . . afternoon,' said Sorrel slowly.

'What did he want to show you when you left me in the café?' Alyse wanted to know.

'Just what he's been doing to the estate to make it pay. Farming's not very profitable nowadays.'

'And what has he been doing?'

'A golf course and a chalet park. We could see them from the shopping courtyard.'

Alyse frowned. 'Why do you think of him as a playboy? He seems very hard-working.'

'Yes.' Sorrel's voice was dreamy. 'Yes, he does, doesn't he?'

'Did you know him well, once upon a time? Sometimes you both act as if you used to be very . . . close.'

Sorrel jumped to her feet. 'Never mind that. You're too tired for long chats. Come on, give me your tray, then lie down and rest.'

★ ★ ★

Alone in the kitchen Sorrel looked out of the window, seeing nothing. 'Sometimes you both act as if you were once very close.' Alyse couldn't know how near she was to the truth.

Giving herself a mental shake, she began to wash the dishes and tidy the kitchen. Work, that was the thing. Find something to occupy her mind.

She dragged a large cardboard box into the shop. It had been waiting to be unpacked for days.

The contents were sufficiently engrossing to take her mind off Marcus Barrington. She had always enjoyed children's books and now sat happily on the floor, lost in the colourful illustrations.

The chimes of the little clock in the kitchen made her jump guiltily to her feet. She must telephone the hospital. Marcus had said an outing would take her mind off Ernst, and for a few hours it had worked. But she didn't want to forget. Poor Ernst.

She dialled the hospital number and

asked to be put through to the ward.

'No change,' she was told, and the words both relieved and depressed her.

She thanked the nurse and went back to her books, but they had lost their charm. Hastily piling them on a shelf in the corner, she went upstairs to the sitting-room.

She sat in the window bay looking out at the fading light over the sea. The seagulls were quiet, while the waves splashed on to the sand, but their sound couldn't be heard through the closed window.

She fingered the glass swan which was still in her pocket, then went to the mantelpiece and lifted down the little wooden swan Ernst had given her that morning. With one finger, she stroked its carved feathers, willing the old man to get better.

A Charming Bavarian

Next morning, Sorrel picked up the telephone to ring the hospital, but before she dialled, on impulse she replaced the receiver and went across to the mantelpiece for the little wooden swan. Cradling it in her hand, she picked up the receiver again and this time dialled.

'Mr Schumann? One moment, please,' The voice was cool and polite. Sorrel waited, stroking the swan's feathers with her thumb.

The nurse returned. 'Miss Basset? You're the lady who visited yesterday? I'm very sorry to have to tell you that Mr Schumann died in the early hours of this morning.'

Sorrel's thumb stopped moving. 'Died?' she said faintly. 'But I thought he was . . . ' She swallowed.

'Mr Schumann was very weak. I'm

sorry. Perhaps you could speak to his nephew? He'll give you more details.'

'His nephew?' Sorrel echoed.

'I believe he's staying at Mr Schumann's house. He's here at the hospital now and will be making all the arrangements. Perhaps you can catch him at home later?'

'Yes, thank you.'

Sorrel replaced the telephone. Ernst — dead. In her heart she had known he wouldn't recover, and yet — she had just hoped for a miracle.

So his nephew had arrived. It would be polite to call later. She hoped he spoke English.

Alyse read the bad news in her face as soon as she saw her and gave her a gentle hug in sympathy.

Breakfast passed in silence. Sorrel didn't want to talk about her old friend just yet.

She was gazing into space, thinking about him, when her glance fell on the clock. 'Goodness, look at the time! I must open up.'

A salesman from a toy company had arranged to call and was already waiting outside. He was large and jolly, a good choice to represent his range of products.

'Morning, morning,' he boomed. 'Just wait till you see this little lot.' He tapped the side of his case. 'Irresistible, I promise you.'

For the next hour, Sorrel was busy with the order and had no time to think about her problems, so that when Alyse brought her a cup of coffee at eleven, she was feeling more composed.

'What are you going to do about the hand-made toys?' asked Alyse.

'Well, obviously there are other toy makers in Cornwall. It's just that I've dealt with Ernst for so long. There's a Craft Fair in Truro next month — I'll see if there's anyone there.'

'There's no immediate rush, though, is there? You have quite a stock of Ernst's toys.'

'Yes, and there may be more in his workshop. And with a bit of luck, his nephew may turn out to be a toy maker.'

'It's not very likely these days,' said Alyse. 'He's more probably a computer programmer.'

Sorrel smiled. 'Well, I shall know this evening. He's here, staying at Ernst's cottage, apparently. I'm going up to see him.'

'Does he know you're coming?'

'No, but I shouldn't imagine he knows anyone in St Towan, so he might be glad to see a friendly face.'

Alyse looked thoughtful. 'I wonder what he's like?' she mused, and gave Sorrel a speculative look.

'Oh, no, don't you go letting your imagination run away with you,' Sorrel warned. 'I should think he'll be too old to interest me.' For if Ernst had been in his eighties, his nephew would probably be in his forties or fifties.

'What did you think of Pencarrock Barns?' Sorrel asked in an effort to change the subject.

For ten minutes they discussed Marcus's ventures.

'I can't think why you're so antagonistic towards him,' Alyse complained, picking up the tray and walking towards the door.

Sorrel grinned. 'What does it matter? You're friendly enough for both of us!' she joked.

When Alyse had gone, she went to the window and looked across the road at the sea. There was a light wind and little choppy waves danced towards the beach.

How could she tell her cousin that she was far from antagonistic towards Marcus Barrington? How could she explain that they had once been close, so close that no-one else could measure up to him. How could she tell her that, and make Alyse feel guilty about her interest in him?

Sighing, she dragged a cardboard box from the little stock-room next door into the centre of the shop floor and set about unpacking its cargo of soft toys, checking them against a list and arranging them in a display basket.

The shop bell rang announcing Tony Redvers' arrival.

'I've just heard about poor old Ernst,' he said. 'I'm sorry.'

'News travels quickly in St Towan!' said Sorrel. 'Have you also heard that his nephew has arrived?'

'No — has he? Perhaps he'll make some wooden toys for you.' He gestured vaguely round the shop.

'Perhaps,' Sorrel agreed, turning back to the box. 'Is this a social visit, because I'm afraid I have a lot to do.'

'Yes, it is, but you might not be interested now. There's a party,' he said, 'tonight — at the cricket club. I wondered if you'd like to go. And Alyse, of course.'

She shook her head. 'I'm not in the party mood. But Alyse might like it. I'll call her.'

Alyse's face lit up at the suggestion of the party, but then she looked uncertainly at Sorrel.

'Don't mind me. You go if you'd like to,' Sorrel assured her, then smiled at

Tony. 'You'll take care of her, won't you?'

'But you can't stay here on your own, Sorrel,' Alyse protested. 'Not — just now . . .'

'I won't. I have plans for this evening.'

'Oh, yes, I forgot — the nephew. Are you really going to see him?'

'Of course. It'll only be a polite visit. Just to say hello and offer my condolences.'

Tony looked at his watch. 'Excuse me — I must be going. I have an appointment in Truro in an hour — a job interview, for which I have high hopes.'

'I thought you were happy where you are?' Tony was manager of a hotel a mile outside St Towan.

'I *was* very happy, but they're closing before Easter, so I'll have to find something else.'

'I couldn't beg a lift, could I?' asked Alyse. 'I'd better go shopping,' she explained to Sorrel. 'I've nothing to wear to a party.'

'How will you get back?'

'I can get the bus. Don't worry about me.'

'I'll bring you back,' Tony put in. 'Would three hours be long enough?'

Sorrel wanted to protest, 'You can't walk around for three hours!' but she held her tongue. Alyse was looking so happy and confident, she didn't want to spoil her mood.

She watched the two go off together, laughing, and thought, if only Alyse could be interested in Tony. She didn't think it would happen, but she could hope.

The shop bell rang and she turned with a welcoming smile to a young couple with two small children.

'We're looking for birthday presents,' explained the mother. 'They're going to a party.'

'Of course — what age is the child?' Sorrel quickly became absorbed; once again her attention was all on her business.

★ ★ ★

60

Alyse arrived back at five laden with carrier bags, her eyes shining. 'We've had a wonderful time,' she said, 'and I've bought so many things.'

'What do you means, 'we'?' I thought Tony had business in Truro?'

'He did, but when he finished, he came shopping with me.'

Sorrel looked at her incredulously. 'Tony Redvers going round dress shops? What *do* you do to men?'

'Don't worry, I shan't take him away from you,' Alyse promised with a mischievous smile.

If only you would, thought Sorrel.

'Why did you need new clothes in such a hurry?' she asked, 'I could have loaned you something for tonight.'

'Well . . . ' Alyse coloured up. 'I seem to be going out a lot more lately.'

'With Marcus?'

'Sometimes. And on my own. And I don't have many clothes — not nice ones, anyway.'

Sorrel smiled at her. 'Give me a minute to lock up and then we'll see what you've bought.'

Perhaps *I* should pay a visit to the Truro dress shops, she thought ruefully, looking down at her working outfit. Black trousers and white blouses weren't exactly exciting. If Alyse had bought some nice clothes, she would look very dull next to her, she mused. And Marcus will notice, she thought involuntarily . . .

She found Alyse excitedly taking garments from brightly-coloured store bags and laying them on the bed for her inspection.

Alyse waved a hand at her display. 'There — what do you think?'

Sorrel picked up a short, pleated skirt in black and white checks.

'Very nice. And what did you get to go with it?'

Alyse held up a white polo-necked jumper. 'This. Or perhaps this.' She picked up another in cerise. 'And I've got some plum trousers to go with these, too.'

Sorrel looked admiringly at a red

dress hanging on the wardrobe door.

'For tonight?' she queried.

'Yes. Tony chose it.'

'You'll be the belle of the ball,' Sorrel returned genuinely. 'What a pity Marcus won't be there to see you.'

'Oh, I don't mind about that.'

'I thought you fancied him?' The words were out before she could stop them.

Alyse raised an eyebrow. 'Marcus? No. He's just a friend. I like him very much, but he's not my type.'

'Oh really? Have you got a type?' Sorrel teased.

Alyse considered. 'Not yet,' she said at last. 'But I'll know him when I meet him.'

'Oh, yes, I forgot. You're looking for a Rhett Butler, aren't you?'

'If I am, I don't think I'll find him in St Towan,' said Alyse with an amused grimace.

★　★　★

The two girls left the shop together at eight. Alyse, in the short red dress edged with gold, set off for the party with Tony, while Sorrel, in sensible trousers and a warm jumper, climbed the hill to Ernst's cottage.

There were lights behind the drawn curtains, so someone, presumably the nephew, was at home.

She walked past the cottage and on up the hill. It was going to be harder than she'd imagined to walk up the path and knock on the door, knowing that a stranger would open it. She leaned against the sea wall. Perhaps it would be better to wait until tomorrow.

But why? Why wait until tomorrow? Resolutely she retraced her steps to the cottage and walked up the path.

The door was opened at her first diffident tap.

'*Ja?*' A young man of medium height with a shock of thick dark hair was looking at her suspiciously.

Sorrel was taken aback. He couldn't be much older than she was.

'Can I help you?' There was a deep, attractive accent but the English was perfect.

'Oh, you speak English.' She was relieved. 'I'm sorry to disturb you but I am — was a friend of your uncle. I wanted to say how sorry I am for your loss — he was a wonderful man — and I wondered if you have made arrangements for the — the funeral.'

He opened the door wider. 'You are Sorrel?' She nodded. 'Please come in.'

She noticed his long sensitive fingers as he closed the door. Perhaps he was a musician.

He turned and smiled. 'My uncle mentioned you many times in his letters. I hoped I would meet you. Sit down, please.'

She sank into a chair near the fire and he sat opposite.

'Did he tell you about me?' he asked.

She shook her head. 'He never said a word about his family. I thought he was alone in the world. He didn't mention where he came from — his home, I mean — until last night.' She looked into the fire. The burning coals, pointed and glowing, reminded her of castles. 'He talked about Bavaria.'

'I have made arrangements to take him back there for burial,' he told her.

'That's what he would have wanted,' Sorrel agreed. 'He spoke so movingly of the forests and castles. I wish he had told me before. We could have talked about them.

'I have made some coffee. You would like a cup?' The young man jumped up and disappeared into the kitchen without waiting for an answer.

'I brought the coffee with me,' he said a little sheepishly as he returned. 'I have had coffee in England before!'

She sipped the dark brown liquid appreciatively. It was delicious — rich and smooth.

'Ach.' He jumped up again. 'I know your name but you do not know mine.' He bowed. 'Carl Schumann.' He sat again and picked up his mug.

Sorrel smiled at him. He was quite charming.

As they drank their coffee in silence, Sorrel felt a sense of peace, almost as if Ernst was there and happy that his two special people had met at last.

'So, you're taking him back to Bavaria. And then?' she asked pleasantly.

'Then?'

'I mean, what will happen to his workshop?'

'I think — I have not yet definitely decided, but I think I shall take it over myself.'

Sorrel was delighted. 'So you're a toy maker too?'

'A woodcarver. Many Bavarians work in wood. It is traditional.'

'Because of all the forests?'

He nodded. 'My uncle wrote that he made you many wooden toys. You have a toyshop, I think?'

'His toys are the most wonderful things I sell. There are many samples in the workshop.'

'Shall we look? You can tell me about them.'

They went into the tidy little room with its orderly array of tools and smell of sawdust and paint. Tears stung Sorrel's eyes when she remembered that Ernst would never use them again.

Carl had taken down some knives and was running a finger expertly along the blade. He nodded approvingly.

'These are good — old, but good.'

He picked up a red and blue clown and smiled as he made it do a comic dance.

'Those are very popular,' Sorrel told him. 'And these.' She handed him a box in the shape of a house with inset pieces which formed the doors and windows.

Together they examined all the brightly-painted toys on the shelf. Carl looked at each one thoughtfully but said nothing until they reached the last toy, a colourful tractor. Then he said, 'Have you many of these in your shop?'

'No. They sell very quickly and there aren't many left. It took Ernst a week to make each one and he would never cut corners.'

'Cut corners?' He was puzzled.

'I'm sorry — I mean, he would never rush anything — do it badly to save time.'

He smiled proudly and nodded. 'A perfectionist.'

'Yes. A perfectionist.'

He led the way back into the sitting-room and they sat again by the fire.

'So what will you do now? Do you know another toy maker?' he wanted to know.

She was puzzled. He had said he might take over the workshop but hadn't offered to make toys for her. Perhaps he had other ideas for his work.

The fire was beginning to sink low. 'There aren't many forests in Cornwall, I think, so I cannot put a log on the fire,' he said.

'No. We make do with coal.' She pointed to the coal scuttle at the side of the fireplace.

'I think I shall leave the fire,' he said. 'Are you hungry? I must go out and find some food. Would you eat with me?'

'That would be nice but I'm afraid I had dinner before I came out. But I'll sit with you while you eat a pasty, if you like.'

'A — pasty? What is a pasty?'

'You've never been to Cornwall before?'

'No. Only to London. Perhaps they do not eat those pasties in London. I have never heard of them.'

'They're traditional Cornish specialities,' she explained. 'They were originally made for the miners to take down the tin mines for their dinners. Now they're made in their thousands, mostly for tourists. But I'm sure you'll enjoy one.'

He looked pleased. 'My first day here, I have a new friend and I am eating traditional food. I like the idea! Come, where do we find these pasties?'

'We'll go to the inn by the harbour,' she said. 'They sell the best.'

It felt odd walking through St Towan with a man who, until two hours ago, had been completely unknown to her. But perhaps because he was Ernst's nephew, he didn't seem like a stranger.

They paused at the bottom of the hill and looked at the sea.

'It must be strange to live with an ocean so close to your house,' he mused. 'I have always lived in the centre of the country. The sea was far away.'

'I've never lived anywhere else,' she said. 'I can't imagine not hearing the splash of the waves when I fall asleep at night and when I wake in the morning.'

He looked around. 'Where is your toyshop?'

She pointed. 'Along there. You must come and see it soon. But we're going this way.' She led the way past the solid granite church and the lifeboat station, across the road and along the harbour road. The sea was quiet. Little boats bobbed at the ends of their mooring lines.

'Do you have storms here?' he asked.

'We certainly do! Sometimes the waves crash right across the road.'

'I think I should like to see that,' he said.

'Here we are.' She led the way into the quaint sixteenth-century inn. She looked nervously round the lounge, dreading to see Marcus or even Pamela. She didn't know Carl well enough yet to introduce him with ease. And yet, she felt a slight frisson of excitement; it might be interesting to let them see her with another man, and obviously on comfortable terms.

Carl was looking around with approval at the low beams and the pewter mugs arranged along shelves where they winked in the flickering light of the huge log fire. The evening was warm but the fire gave the lounge a cheery look.

They gave their order and chose a table in a secluded corner. There were few people in the lounge, most preferring the noisy companionship of the bar, but Sorrel wanted privacy for their conversation.

Carl took a long swig of his beer and sat back with a sigh of satisfaction.

'This is pleasant. When I arrived in your country, I thought I would have a lonely time. Now already I have a friend.' He beamed at her.

She was saved from having to reply by the arrival of his pasty. He was obviously hungry, and she watched with amusement as he demolished the first with enthusiasm and ordered another.

'Very good,' he declared. 'When I go home I think I shall open a pasty shop.'

She laughed — but then realised what he had said.

'When you go home? But I thought you were going to take over your uncle's workshop?'

'Ach, the businesswoman. You think of your toyshop.'

She shrugged. 'Of course. I must

have my supply of wooden toys. People expect them.'

'There are many things to consider,' he said seriously. 'My uncle loved it here. I must see exactly what he found so fascinating.' He smiled at the waitress as she put his second pasty in front of him. 'So far, I am very pleased with what I have seen.' He gave her a meaningful look and she blushed.

'You seem very young to have an uncle of Ernst's age,' she commented to cover her embarrassment.

'Actually he was my great-uncle, my grandfather's brother,' Carl explained.

'Why did he decide to live in England?' she asked. 'He loved his homeland so much, why did he leave?'

Carl wiped the greasy crumbs from his mouth and took another drink of his beer before he answered.

'He had no choice. He was conscripted into the army.'

She nodded. 'Yes, I realise that, but when the war was over, why didn't he go back?'

Carl sighed. 'It was very sad. He had a girl — his childhood sweetheart. Always the dream was that they would marry and settle in their village. But he became a prisoner of war and was sent to work on farms in England. He was lonely, but he had the dream — marriage to Hannelore, a family, his own workshop.' He paused, then continued: 'But . . . he was gone so long. Hannelore met someone else. She wrote that she could not wait for him. She was married.'

'Oh, poor Ernst! To hear that when he was so far from home!'

Carl nodded. 'But he became friendly with a girl who worked with him on the farm. When the war was over, they married and returned to her home in Cornwall.'

'In St Towan?'

'No. Another small town. I do not know the name. But they were not happy. So he moved here and never left.'

'But he could have lived somewhere

else in Bavaria,' she pressed. 'At least he would have been in his homeland.'

Carl smiled. 'How can we know how other people feel? He didn't want to go back, that is what he said.'

They were both silent, thinking of the lonely old man, living by himself, creating his beautiful toys. Perhaps he had thought he could never trust women again.

Sorrel thought of herself and Marcus. She had been so badly hurt that she felt she could no longer trust men. Was it possible for her to change? She didn't want to spend the rest of her life like Ernst, with no-one to love — and no-one to love her.

'You have always lived in this town?' asked Carl.

'Mm. My parents had a shop here — groceries, not toys.'

'They still live here?'

'No. They're in Australia.'

'Australia!' He sounded amazed. 'But that is on the other side of the world.'

She laughed. 'It certainly is. My

brother got married, went to live there and had two children. My mother wanted to be near her grandchildren to see them grow up, so she and my father emigrated last year.'

'Leaving you alone?' He sounded appalled.

'But I'm not alone,' she protested. 'My cousin Alyse lives with me.'

'You did not want to go to Australia with your family?'

'No. I have my shop. Ever since I was a little girl, I've wanted a toyshop — and now I have one,' she said proudly.

'I should like to see this toyshop.'

'It would be best for you to see it in daylight. Shall we go for a stroll around the town, or are you too tired after your journey here?'

'I am tired,' he admitted, 'but I would like to see something of my uncle's town.' He stood up and gave her his hand, drawing her to her feet.

By now, some of the other tables were occupied and she received interested glances from people who knew her. By tomorrow all of St Towan would know that Sorrel Basset had been seen out with a strange young man, and probably it would also know that he was the nephew of Ernst, the toy maker.

When they left the inn darkness was falling and lights dotted along the harbour and around the town gave it a magical look.

Carl breathed deeply. 'What a wonderful smell! Salt and sea and fish and I don't know what else. It is very foreign to me.'

Sorrel laughed. 'We think of foreign as things which are strange to us. But to you foreign is things which are familiar to us.'

'That is very clever,' he said solemnly. 'Very deep.'

'It's not,' she protested. 'It's probably quite silly. Come on, I'll show you some of the town before it gets too dark. You can have a proper look tomorrow in daylight.'

They climbed to the top of the main

street to the carpark overlooking a wide beach. It was dark by now. The sea looked inky black, but the lights caught the frothy underside of the waves as they creamed on to the beach. Sorrel shivered as the breeze tugged at her hair.

'You permit?' asked Carl and slipped an arm round her shoulders. She didn't reply, but neither did she pull away. His arm was comforting.

They began the descent to the street again, and once away from the wind she gently moved from his protective arm.

'These are the main shops of the town,' she said. 'It's all very small as you can see. But we have everything we need.'

'And you have your big town nearby, the town where my uncle was in hospital.'

'Truro, yes. But it's hardly a big town — it's more of a small city. It has a grand cathedral.'

'Perhaps you would show it to me one day.'

This was going rather fast, thought Sorrel suddenly. I need time to collect my thoughts. Carl's very charming but I know nothing about him. I've only known him a few hours. So what am I doing walking round these deserted streets with him in the dark? For a sensible woman, I've behaved rather stupidly. But he is Ernst's nephew . . .

This argument with herself was interrupted by her companion. 'You look very thoughtful,' he commented.

She smiled. 'It's nothing.'

They had reached the bottom of the hill and Sorrel pointed to the right. 'Your cottage is up there. I have to go this way. I'm sure we'll see each other again soon.'

'Thank you for your company.' He took her hand and bowed formally. 'May I telephone and tell you the arrangements for the funeral?'

'Please do, though I'm afraid I shan't be able to come, not to Bavaria.'

'I would not expect it. You have a business to run.'

With smiles, they parted, and Sorrel walked the last few yards to her home, her thoughts in a whirl.

Alyse was home and already in her dressing-gown.

'I was beginning to think you were staying out all night!' she joked. 'Where have you been — and who has put that flush in your cheeks? You look happier than I've seen you for ages!'

'I've had a very strange evening,' said Sorrel. 'How about you? Did you enjoy yourself?'

'It was great fun! But never mind that just now — I want to know about the nephew.'

'Great-nephew actually.'

'Oh. So he's not as old as you thought he'd be?'

'No. I think he's about my age.'

'So the flush on your cheeks . . . '

'That was the wind,' said Sorrel. Then she relented. 'Oh, all right, I'll tell you all about him . . . '

A Bolt From The Blue

The rotor blades of the helicopter overhead made such a clatter that Alyse almost dropped the toy she was examining. Then there was a scream from the street outside —

With Sorrel she rushed to the window to see a small group of people gathered round a figure on the ground, and a big black horse on the other side of the road, tossing his head and being soothed by a competent-looking young girl.

'Open the door!' shouted a familiar voice and Tony Redvers rushed in with Pamela Barrington in his arms. 'Darned helicopter,' he said. 'It startled the horse and it threw her.'

'Bring her through to my room.' Alyse hurried to open the bedroom door and Tony gently lowered Pamela on to the bed. She groaned as her shoulder hit the bed.

Gently Tony removed her riding boots. 'Send for Dr Main,' he said over his shoulder.

Sorrel hurried to the telephone and dialled the surgery. The doctor was out but his receptionist would contact him and he would be right over.

Pamela was very pale, her skin milky-white against her red hair, but her eyes were open and she was quite conscious. She made no noise but winced every time she moved her shoulder.

'Shouldn't we send for Marcus?' Alyse suggested.

'Oh, my goodness, yes!' said Sorrel. 'Where can we reach him?' she asked Pamela.

'He'll be at the Barns,' she said faintly. 'If he's not there, he could be anywhere.'

Sorrel went back to the telephone and dialled the number Pamela had given her. There was no answer.

'I'll try again in a moment,' she told the others.

'Could we make her a cup of tea, do you think?' suggested Alyse.

'No. Nothing till the doctor gets here,' said Tony.

As he gently brushed a fall of hair from Pamela's eyes, Sorrel watched him, surprised. This gentle, attentive man was very different from the carefree, devil-may-care Tony she knew so well. Was it something about Pamela herself that was bring out this softer side to him?

The arrival of Dr Main put an end to her musings. Asking only Alyse to remain, he sent the others from the room.

'Dr Main has seen quite a lot of Alyse since she's been here,' Sorrel explained to Tony. 'I expect that's why he asked her to stay.'

He nodded. 'And she's a sweet, gentle girl,' he said, 'just the right person to look after someone who needs TLC.'

'I must get back to the shop,' Sorrel commented. 'Make yourself a coffee if you like.'

He considered, then shook his head.

'I think I'd better take a look at that horse,' he said. 'Young Jenna Maitland is doing a great job of soothing him, but I think I should get him back to his stable all the same. I can't understand why Pamela was riding him.'

She looked at him questioningly.

'Don't you recognise him?' he queried. 'Great black brute! It's Marcus's horse, Nansen. He's much too powerful for Pamela, however good a horsewoman she is.'

Sorrel crossed to the window. 'He looks quiet enough now.'

'Mm. It's lucky he's a large horse, he'll manage my weight.'

'Watch he doesn't throw you too.'

Tony patted her shoulder. 'Don't worry about me.'

'How will you get back from Pencarrock?' she wondered.

'Someone will drive me, I'm sure. Perhaps Marcus is there. If he is, I can explain about Pamela.'

She watched as Tony crossed the road, spoke to Jenna, then hoisted himself into the saddle. She frowned in concern. He was wearing his ordinary clothes, and no hard hat. Pamela's wouldn't have fitted him. She hoped he would be all right and that nothing else would startle the horse.

Dr Main came out of the bedroom. 'She's a lucky girl. No real damage. She's wrenched that shoulder but it's not broken or dislocated. I can't understand how she escaped more serious injuries.'

'So we can give her a cup of tea?'

He nodded. 'Marcus can take her up to the hospital for an X-ray if it'll make him feel happier, but there's no need. I'll call at Pencarrock tomorrow to make sure she's all right. Thank you for your help, young lady,' he said to Alyse as she appeared at the bedroom door. 'I know I'm leaving her in good hands.'

Alyse looked pleased. 'I'll make her a cup of tea,' she said, 'with extra sugar. That'll set her right.'

Sorrel went out to the street and

looked up and down. There were no potential customers in sight. For once that was good news. It meant she had time to phone Marcus.

She went back inside, picked up the telephone and dialled his number. He answered on the third ring and sounded distracted, as though he was busy with something.

'Hello — Marcus Barrington.'

'Marcus, it's Sorrel. You haven't seen Tony Redvers, have you?'

'Tony Redvers? No, why?'

Briefly she related the events of the past hour. 'But don't worry — she's resting and Alyse is with her.'

'I can't leave here for an hour or so.' Marcus sounded concerned. 'But I'll come and get her as soon as I can.'

'Don't worry,' Sorrel said again. 'We'll look after her.'

She replaced the receiver and glanced at the clock. Ten minutes and she would close for lunch.

She tidied the rack of books and picked up pieces of Lego from the floor around the table where children were allowed to play, and she was straightening the little chairs when the clock chimed one. Thankfully she reversed the sign on the door. Better go and see how the invalid was getting on.

Pamela was sitting on the couch in the living-room. Her face was still very white, but she gave Sorrel a wan smile.

'Thanks for letting me rest here,' she said. 'Your cousin has been very kind.'

Alyse flushed and busied herself pouring tea for them.

'Have you contacted Marcus?' Pamela asked.

'Yes. He said he should be here in about an hour.'

Silence fell. Sorrel ate the sandwiches Alyse had prepared for her lunch and Pamela sipped her tea. There had never been friendship between the two girls, even when Sorrel and Marcus had been so close. Pamela's attitude was that no one, least of all a humble shopkeeper, was good enough for her brother.

We can't sit in silence until Marcus

comes, thought Sorrel, desperately searching for something to talk about.

'We enjoyed the visit to your restaurant,' she said at last. 'It's very attractive. Was the colour scheme your idea?'

'Yes. Marcus left it all to me. It's been quite a success, I must say. But I'm not going to be there much longer.'

'Oh? Are you leaving St Towan?'

'No, I'm starting my own business. I'm opening a wine bar. Didn't Marcus tell you?'

'No. Why should he?'

Pamela gave a sly smile and looked around the room. 'If he hasn't mentioned it, I don't know whether I should.'

'Please yourself. It's your affair.'

Alyse came in from the kitchen with a plate of cakes, put them on the table and sat down. She must have sensed an atmosphere because she looked from one girl to the other.

'You'll have to know sooner or later,' Pamela finally said. 'The lease on your shop won't be renewed; I'm having it for my wine bar.'

The cousins stared at her, speechless. Sorrel was the first to recover. 'You're joking!'

'I should think the sooner you know the better,' said Pamela. 'After all, you'll need to make other arrangements.'

'But why this shop?' asked Alyse. 'Surely there are other empty properties in St Towan?'

'There's old Ernst's cottage for one. It has a workshop at the back. Plenty of room for conversion,' Sorrel pointed out, sounding desperate.

'Not suitable,' Pamela drawled. 'No, this place will be perfect. Look at the position, right opposite the sea. Very atmospheric.'

Sorrel felt as if she had been crushed. She looked at Alyse and saw her misery reflected in her cousin's eyes.

'And when was this decided?' Her voice was quiet.

'Quite recently. I went to stay with a friend in London who has just opened a wine bar and I thought, what a good idea! It's just what St Towan needs. Give it a younger image.'

'So you decided to take my toyshop,' Sorrel said, her voice flat.

'A toyshop doesn't have to be atmospheric. It's just a shop. We'll find you somewhere else.' Pamela looked round the room with a proprietorial air. 'Stainless steel and driftwood,' she said, 'a mixture of old and new. I can see it now.'

There was a knock on the outer door. Sorrel went to open it. It was Marcus. Silently she let him in, relocked the door and led the way into the sitting-room. She said nothing. Alyse nodded to him but also said nothing. He couldn't help but notice the strained atmosphere. He looked around at the three women.

'Why the silence? I thought you said she was all right?' He looked at his sister who smiled sweetly.

'It's shock, darling. I discovered that they didn't know about the wine bar, so

I've just told them.'

Marcus looked from his sister to Sorrel and back again, horror evident in his expression.

'You haven't! You had no right. I was going to discuss it with Sorrel myself.'

Pamela, realising how angry Marcus was, sought to justify herself.

'She needs time to make other arrangements. It's not fair to keep her in the dark.'

'Sorrel.' Marcus turned to her. 'Look, I'm sorry. I really didn't mean you to find out this way. I tried to talk to you at the Schooner but you wouldn't listen.'

'You've seen me since then,' she pointed out, her tone hostile.

'Yes, but not alone. It isn't something you can just throw out over the lunch table. Anyway, I wanted you to enjoy that afternoon.'

'What a fuss about nothing,' protested Pamela. 'A decision has been made. We'll find you somewhere else, don't worry.'

'Fuss about nothing?' Sorrel echoed bitterly. 'It may be nothing to you, but it's my life's dream to me. I've worked hard to establish it here. People know where it is. Do you realise that I get customers from as far away as Falmouth? Ernst's toys are famous.'

'Yes, well — he's not around now, is he, so that's the end of that,' Pamela returned. She had never been much troubled by sentiment.

Sorrel sat down heavily. Tears threatened, but she would not cry in front of the Barringtons.

Marcus looked at his sister and his expression was far from affectionate. 'We'd better be going. Can you walk?'

'Yes. Is the car outside? I'll be glad to get home.'

As Alyse went ahead to open the door for them, Marcus turned to Sorrel. 'I just don't know how . . .'

She waved a dismissive hand at him, went into the kitchen and closed the door. Without another word, the Barringtons left the shop.

★ ★ ★

Alyse went back into the kitchen, took a bottle from the cupboard and poured a tot of brandy for her cousin.

Sorrel tried to refuse, but Alyse insisted. 'Right now you need something stronger than tea. You can suck a mint before you go back to work to disguise the smell of it on your breath.'

Sorrel sipped the brandy and stared into space.

'I'm not sticking up for Marcus,' Alyse began hesitantly, 'but he did try to tell you at the Schooner. And it's not his fault Pamela is so bitchy and blurted it out.'

'There won't be anywhere else,' said Sorrel, as if she hadn't heard. 'I don't know of any vacant properties in St Towan that would do.'

'What about Ernst's place?'

'Carl may stay. And it would need a lot of alterations. I can't afford it. I've spent everything getting this place just right.' A tear slid down her cheek but she furiously wiped it away. Crying wouldn't help. She must think. But not right now; right now she must open the shop again.

★   ★   ★

After dinner, Sorrel and Alyse returned again to the subject of Pamela and the wine bar.

'Why does Marcus give in to her?' asked Alyse. 'She's so spoilt.'

'She had some serious illness as a small child and nearly died,' Sorrel explained. 'Because of that, and the fact that her mother was dead, everyone spoiled her, especially her father. He idolised her. Everything she wanted, she got. Probably he expected that after his death, Marcus would carry on spoiling her.'

'Is Marcus older than her?'

'Yes, by about three years.'

'It'll be a good thing when she finds a husband and he can take over. Give Marcus a break.'

'Did you notice the way Tony Redvers looked at her?' asked Sorrel after a moment.

'Mm. *And* the way she looked at him. Perhaps you're losing your boyfriend,' Alyse mused.

'Friend, not *boy* friend,' Sorrel corrected. 'But I'm not sure I'd want any friend of mine to marry Pamela. I think it would be the end of my friendship with Tony.'

'I don't think you have to worry about that. From what you say about her, she'll think Tony isn't good enough for her,' Alyse pointed out.

The telephone rang and Sorrel went to answer it. She was back within a few minutes, her face slightly flushed.

'That was Carl Schumann,' she said. 'He wants to come over. I told him to give us half an hour.'

Alyse looked satisfied. 'Good. I'd like to meet him.' She stood up and began to clear the table. 'I'll do this while you go and change out of those boring shop clothes. Get into something glamorous before he comes.'

Sorrel opened her mouth to argue, thought better of it, and meekly went upstairs.

Alyse gave her an approving glance when she came back down wearing a blue jumper and blue striped trousers, her hair loose about her shoulders. 'That's better!'

Carl arrived a few minutes later. 'You were just in time,' Alyse murmured with a smile to her cousin as she went to open the door.

Carl gave a little bow and handed her a small bunch of freesias. 'For you.'

Sorrel took him through to the sitting-room and introduced him to Alyse who received the same greeting and flowers.

She buried her face in their petals. 'Lovely.' She smiled. 'My favourites.'

She took both bunches into the kitchen and returned with them in two crystal vases. Sorrel had seated Carl in an armchair near the fire where he sat smiling around at the room.

'Charming,' he said. 'I have not been in many English homes.'

'Would you like a cup of coffee?' asked Alyse.

'Carl brings his own coffee,' Sorrel confided with a chuckle. 'He doesn't approve of English coffee.'

'Please.' He put up a hand in protest. 'Thank you, *Fräulein* Alyse, I should love some.'

As Alyse disappeared again into the kitchen, Carl smiled at Sorrel. 'Will you show me your shop. You promised.'

It was on the tip of her tongue to reply that there wasn't much point, that her shop would soon be no more, but she felt that she didn't know him well enough to discuss her private affairs.

She led the way to the shop, switched on the light and stood back for him to enter.

As the room sprang into light, illuminating the bright paintwork and neatly arranged toys and books, she felt a pang of heartache. How much longer would all this, her pride and joy, be hers?

She swallowed hard and bit her lip to regain her composure. Carl hadn't noticed anything. He was entranced by the toys in the window.

'Uncle Ernst's toys,' he said softly. 'They look very good.'

'They are,' she agreed. 'I can't believe there'll be no more. Unless,' she looked hopefully at him, 'unless you . . . '

He turned towards her, seemed about to speak, then changed his mind and walked over to a shelf of toy vehicles.

'I loved to play with toy cars when I was young,' he said, picking up a red racing car and spinning the wheels with his finger tip.

Sorrel was puzzled. If he wanted to settle in St Towan, surely he should be pleased to have a ready market for his toys? Why didn't he want to discuss it? This wasn't the first time he had shied away from the topic.

'The coffee will be ready,' she said, moving away from the door.

With a last look round, Carl followed

her. 'It's a beautiful shop,' he said. 'You must be very proud.'

Emotion welled in her and she couldn't reply.

When they were settled with their coffees, she asked him about Ernst's funeral.

'I'm taking him home tomorrow,' he said. 'The hospital has been very helpful and made many of the arrangements for me. I'm very grateful.'

'And when is the funeral to be?'

'In five days. In my village we have the most beautiful white and gold church. The service will be held there. When I return, I shall bring you a photograph of the church.'

Sorrel moved to a little table in the corner and picked up an envelope which she handed to Carl.

'Please buy flowers from Alyse and me,' she said. 'There is money in here and a card to put with them. I don't know his favourite flowers, but perhaps something bright like his lovely painted toys?'

Carl smiled gently and put the envelope in his inside pocket. 'Of course,' he nodded.

'When will you be back?' asked Alyse.

'I hope in the middle of next week,' he answered. 'I shall find it hard to stay away now that I have made such charming friends.' He glanced at his watch. 'I think I must go. I must make preparations for the morning.'

A loud knock at the door made them all jump.

'Who can that be? It's kind of late for callers,' said Sorrel, getting up and going to the door.

On the doorstep stood Marcus Barrington. They stared at each other without speaking for a few seconds, then Marcus put out a hand and touched her arm. 'Sorrel, I'm sorry it's late but I didn't want this to go on any longer. We *must* talk.'

'"This" being your decision to take my shop away from me, I suppose,' she returned icily.

He looked stricken. 'I'm so sorry you

had to hear it from Pamela, and so abruptly. She's very sorry too.'

I'm sure she is, thought Sorrel bitterly. She *enjoyed* telling me.

'You'd better come in. We can't talk here.'

In the sitting-room, Carl had stood up ready to take his leave. When Marcus entered, he hesitated in surprise, and the two men stared at each other, weighing each other up. Sorrel performed brief introductions and they shook hands, but there was a wariness between them.

Alyse, watching, thought that Marcus was wondering what this foreigner was doing on obviously friendly terms with Sorrel, and Carl was suspicious that Marcus, who seemed to know her well, was calling so late. It was a typical display of masculine rivalry, she thought to herself with a little smile.

'Carl's just leaving,' said Sorrel and walked him to the door. She made the right comments on the coming sad occasion, but half her mind remained with Marcus. What had he come to say?

She returned to the room where Alyse and Marcus were sitting in awkward silence. Loyalty to her cousin made Alyse view Marcus's actions with suspicion, and yet she liked him so much.

The conflicting feelings embarrassed her and she was glad when Sorrel took him upstairs to her sitting-room and she could concentrate on her embroidery, an activity she invariably found soothing.

By now, it was dark outside. Sorrel drew the curtains and switched on the electric fire. Marcus was watching her in silence. She gestured him to a chair and sat opposite, waiting for him to speak. He seemed not to know how to start.

'I can't tell you how sorry I am that you had to hear about the lease from Pamela. She had no right to tell you like that, and yet — ' he paused ' — she had every right to tell you.'

Sorrel waited. He was talking in

riddles. What did he mean?

'You regard me as your landlord,' he went on. 'I've always dealt with the shop in that capacity. But in fact it's Pamela who owns the property.'

'Pamela?'

'Yes. She owns all of those properties in St Towan which belong to the family. When my father died, he bequeathed Pencarrock and the estate to me and the properties in the town to Pamela. I administer them for her but when she marries she'll take them over herself.'

Sorrel looked from him to the artificially flickering flames of the fire.

'I think her wine bar idea is a good one,' he admitted. 'It'll give her something to really get involved in — the restaurant is mine, after all — but I don't agree with her taking your shop. I'm sure there must be somewhere else. I've argued with her about it but she's adamant.'

Sorrel turned her head and looked at him. 'Then why have you come to discuss it? It's a fait accompli, isn't it?

Pamela wants my shop and intends to have it.'

'Please don't be bitter,' he appealed. 'I'll do everything I can to find you somewhere else.'

While Sorrel sat deep in thought, Marcus watched her, a concerned look on his face. He was about to speak again when she took a deep breath and stood up.

'How long do I have?'

'There's no hurry,' he said anxiously. 'Pamela has to get plans drawn up and builders organised. And get a manager, of course.'

'I see.' She bent and switched off the fire. The interview was plainly over. Marcus looked as if he would like to talk longer, but she opened the door and led the way downstairs.

'Thank you again for your care of Pamela this morning,' he said.

'I hope she's more comfortable now.'

'She was very lucky not to break something. I'm sure she'll soon be back to her old self.'

Sorrel gave a tiny smile and opened the street door. 'Thank you for coming to tell me about the lease,' she said formally.

'I'll be in touch as soon as I have some news,' he promised.

Sorrel closed the door and leaned against it. So that was that. She could do nothing until she heard again from the Barringtons. But one thing was certain, she was going to lose her shop.

Alyse's bedroom door opened and she peeped out like a mouse from a hole. 'Well?'

Sorrel gave her a weak smile. 'You can come out. He's gone.'

'What did he have to say? Is there any hope?'

'I don't know whether there's any point in discussing it, but I'll tell you what he said. But, Alyse, this must make no difference to your friendship with Marcus. This problem is between Pamela and me.'

'We Were Inseparable...'

Sorrel turned off the main road into the lane that led to Penrose, the beautiful old house where Nicole and Carreg Madron lived. Carreg was a doctor at the local hospital and ran Penrose as a convalescent home for young children. Nicole, a former ballet dancer and now a dance teacher in the town, helped him with dance therapy for the children. She and Sorrel were close friends.

Nicole had rung soon after breakfast.

'Sorrel, do you have any more of those small, soft balls? You know, the ones they can squeeze in their hands?' she had asked.

'Yes, I'm sure I have. How many do you want?'

'Twenty if you have them,' Nicole returned. 'And I have a list of some other things . . . '

Sorrel had noted down the selection

of items, and then Nicole had asked, 'Are you busy today, or could you come to lunch? I haven't seen you for ages.'

'Donna's here so I could get away,' Sorrel had returned. 'I'll bring the toys with me.'

Donna Stewart was a small, sandy-haired Scotswoman in her thirties, hard-working and always cheerful, who came in once a week to do the housework Alyse couldn't manage, and once a week to run the shop and give Sorrel a break.

Penrose wasn't far up the lane. She turned into the gateway and swept round the circular drive. The gentle autumn sun caught the small-paned windows of the house and made them sparkle.

Children's laughter bubbled out from the gardens at the side. Penrose was a happy place and Sorrel loved to visit.

She went up the steps to where the front door was standing open. The big, cool hall was empty. She admired, as she always did, the elegant blue carpet and rich cream paintwork.

'Hello? Anyone home?' she called and the housekeeper came hurrying from the dining-room.

'Good morning, Miss Basset. Mrs Madron is in the playroom. I'll take you through.'

Sorrel smiled. 'Don't trouble yourself, Mrs Fry. You must be busy. I can find my way.'

At the rear of the house, a large room had been extended into the garden. Its huge windows gave a wide view of the flowerbeds and fountains which had been the pride and joy of Carreg's grandmother when she had occupied the house. Each wall was painted a different primary colour, and small tables and chairs and cupboards full of toys made it a children's paradise.

Sorrel paused in the doorway and watched the activity in progress. Eight or nine small children with paper wings attached to their shoulders were fluttering and bouncing around the room under the watchful eye of a slim,

109

graceful girl in a pale blue leotard. She looked up, caught Sorrel's eye and waved.

'Only a few minutes more,' she called.

The girls had met two years before when Nicole and Carreg had set up the convalescent home for children and visited Sorrel's shop for toys. Sorrel and Nicole had become firm friends, though their busy lives made it difficult to meet often.

The music ended and the children flopped on to the floor, and as Sorrel applauded the little dancers they laughed self-consciously.

'Very good, butterflies,' Nicole encouraged. 'We'll do it again tomorrow.'

She gestured to two young assistants to take over, and turned to her friend.

'It's lovely to see you. It's been ages!' She shrugged on a long woollen cardigan then linked her arm through the other girl's. 'Come and have a coffee and tell me all your news.'

They were soon settled in comfy armchairs in the big, sunny drawing-room. Mrs Fry brought in a tray of coffee and home-made biscuits, while two small boys who had followed her stood in the doorway watching Sorrel with large, expressive eyes.

'Would you take them back to the playroom, please, Mrs Fry?' said Nicole. 'They hate to miss anything,' she added to Sorrel. 'And visitors are especially interesting!'

She poured the coffee and as she handed a cup to Sorrel, she looked at her intently. 'Are you all right? You look a bit — I don't know — solemn.'

Sorrel gave her a wan smile and Nicole gasped, suddenly remembering.

'Of course — your friend, the old toy maker, died, didn't he? No wonder you feel sad.'

Sorrel nodded. 'It was a shock, although, of course, he was old and hadn't been well.'

'But I hear his nephew is a wood carver or something of the sort, so perhaps he'll take over.'

Sorrel looked surprised. 'How did you hear about Carl? He's only been here a few days.'

'You know St Towan — everyone knows everything!' said Nicole with a mischievous grin.

'Well, here's something you won't know,' said Sorrel. 'I shan't need another toy maker because I won't have a shop.'

Nicole blinked. 'You're giving up?'

'Not me. But Marcus Barrington isn't going to renew my lease — or rather, he's allowing his sister not to renew it.'

'But Marcus isn't like that!' Nicole said, frowning. 'We know him — he's very nice.'

Sorrel grinned. 'I don't think you'd feel that way if he was your landlord and had the power to take *your* life away from you!'

Nicole put out a hand in protest. 'Sorrel, that's a bit melodramatic.'

Sorrel shook her head. 'Not to me. My shop *is* my life. I've put everything into it for the last few years.'

'Can you find somewhere else? I

know it wouldn't be the same, but . . . '

'Marcus has promised to help with that, but I'm sure there isn't anywhere in St Towan.'

'Where does Pamela come into it?'

'I've just discovered that she owns all the shops and houses in St Towan which belong to the Barringtons, and she wants my shop for a wine bar. To be fair to Marcus, he can't do anything about it.'

'I don't mean to pry but — weren't you and Marcus quite friendly once? I'm sure I heard something . . . '

'Did Marcus tell you?'

'Oh no, he's never discussed you. He wouldn't do anything like that,' Nicole declared stoutly, and Sorrel gave her a wry smile.

'You have a very good opinion of him.'

Nicole shrugged. 'I have no reason not to have. He and Carreg are great friends and we see quite a lot of him. He seems to be lonely, despite that demanding sister of his.'

'Lonely!' The disbelief was unmistakable in Sorrel's voice.

'Well, he doesn't play the field, does he?' Nicole defended him. 'And he's very attractive.'

Sorrel said nothing, and Nicole jumped to her feet.

'Come on — you need cheering up! It's a lovely morning. Shall we walk down to the terrace and see if there are any seals? Lunch won't be for another hour.'

They sauntered through the flower-filled gardens, down a twisting path, towards the cliff-top terrace. Chairs were grouped around a table, and thick shrubs on either side sheltered it from sea winds. Settling themselves, they looked out towards the sea.

'You didn't answer my question,' Nicole prompted gently.

'Question? Oh, about Marcus and me? I can't believe you haven't heard already.'

Nicole waited expectantly and Sorrel gave a deep sigh. It looked like she wasn't going to get out of it.

'It was before you came to St Towan. For a year, Marcus and I were . . . well, inseparable. He was the love of my life,' she said simply. 'But I wasn't of his apparently.' Plucking a leaf, she began to twist it in her fingers. 'He married someone else.'

Nicole put a sympathetic hand on her arm. 'I knew he'd been married for a short while. I didn't know you were involved.'

'The estate needed a lot of money spending on it,' Sorrel said quietly. 'I imagine his father didn't approve of me — no money, after all! — so he introduced Marcus to the daughter of a friend, a Brazilian millionaire, would you believe? She was beautiful and Marcus was young and easily influenced.'

'But he loved you!'

Sorrel shrugged. 'Did he? Anyway, he was persuaded that his duty was to the estate and his family.'

Nicole was appalled. 'I don't believe

it! It sounds like the plot of a historical novel. No one behaves like that these days — do they?'

'You'd think not. But his father was an exceptionally forceful character. It would have taken a stronger man than Marcus to stand up to him.'

Nicole considered all this for a moment, then commented, 'Obviously the marriage didn't last.'

'No. His . . . wife was unhappy and homesick. I didn't speak to Marcus again, so I don't know how he felt. But after a year, she went back to Brazil. I assume they got a divorce.'

'How do you know all this if you didn't speak to him?' Nicole wondered.

'Donna Stewart's friend was a cook at Pencarrock. She told Donna, and Donna used to pass on the gossip.'

'But you stayed in love with him?' Nicole probed gently.

'Certainly not!' The answer came too quickly. She turned away so that Nicole couldn't see the hurt in her eyes. 'I wrote him a letter after we broke up. It was foolish, I suppose, but I was young and very hurt. I told him that I hoped he would be happy — and I did mean it, because I loved him — but that he had broken my heart. And that I never wanted to speak to him again. I do speak to him occasionally now, of course, but only out of politeness or for business.'

'What did he do about the letter?' Nicole wanted to know.

'Nothing. That made it worse. He just ignored it.' She turned and this time her friend could see the tears. 'That shows what he really thought of me, doesn't it?'

'Look, over there.' Nicole pointed to a cave in the cliffs opposite. 'Two adult seals and a baby.'

Sorrel was momentarily distracted. 'Where? Oh, yes, on the rocks. Aw, isn't the baby seal sweet?'

They stood up to see better. The sea breeze blew strands of hair across Sorrel's face. Nicole put her arm round the other girl's shoulders.

'Come on,' she said gently. 'Lunch will be ready. Let's go back.'

'I'm sorry to spoil the day with my miseries,' said Sorrel, 'but it's good to talk to someone. I can't tell Alyse.'

Slowly they retraced their steps to the house.

'Why can't you tell Alyse?' Nicole wondered, and Sorrel sighed.

'It's complicated. She's become friendly with Marcus recently. Of course, she knows nothing about our 'history'. I don't know whether there's anything more than friendship — they both say there isn't — but I can't talk to her about my relationship with him. It doesn't seem fair to influence her.'

Nicole stopped and put both hands on Sorrel's shoulders, gazing into her friend's sorrowful eyes.

'I think you do still care for him,' she said simply. 'Why don't you admit it? I can help.'

'No!' Sorrel was alarmed. 'Please don't say anything to anyone. All this is confidential. Promise, Nicole! Promise

118

you won't say anything to Marcus or Carreg.'

Nicole regarded her for a moment before nodding. 'All right, I promise.'

They resumed their walk.

'I'll work something out,' said Sorrel. 'I might even join my family in Australia.' She gave a forced laugh. 'If I don't have my shop, I'll be free to do anything, won't I?'

Nicole said nothing. She knew what the shop meant to Sorrel. She was thinking furiously. Was there anything she could do to help if she wasn't to discuss it with Marcus or Carreg? She was convinced that Sorrel still loved Marcus, and if his lack of interest in other girls meant anything, he still loved Sorrel, too. She discounted his interest in Alyse. Alyse was an appealing girl who brought out the protective instinct in men. Marcus couldn't help wanting to look after her, but as a woman she wasn't his type. Sorrel was, and their romance must be re-kindled.

She opened the door and they

entered the house. 'Come on, one of Mrs Fry's special chicken and mush-room pies will cheer you up. I know they're your favourites.'

Sorrel smiled gratefully. She wanted to change the subject from the agonis-ing one of her and Marcus.

'Will Carreg be back for lunch?' she asked.

'No, he's out all day today.'

They made their way to the dining-room and the appetising smell of chicken pie.

★ ★ ★

Two hours later, Sorrel walked down the main street of St Towan from the car park, carrying the box which had held the toys but was now filled with apples and new-laid eggs. Penrose produced a wide range of foodstuffs and Nicole was generous with them.

She turned the corner at the bottom to see a tall figure walking away from the shop. Marcus. Had he come to see her — or Alyse? She slowed her steps so that he could get far away before she turned into the shop doorway.

'Sorrel — you're back. How's Nicole?' Alyse made a space on the kitchen table and began to unpack the box.

'She's fine,' Sorrel answered automatically. 'Did I see Marcus leaving the shop?'

'Yes. He came to see us. He said it wasn't anything important — he just wanted to see how we were.' Alyse washed an apple and bit into it with relish.

'Guilty conscience, I expect,' Sorrel commented, sounding bitter.

'Please, Sorrel — it really isn't his fault,' Alyse appealed. 'You know what Pamela's like. And she does own the property.'

Donna came out of the stock-room at that moment and Sorrel chose to change the subject. She didn't want to discuss recent events with the older woman.

'Would you like some apples for the

twins?' she asked her. Donna's twin boys were her pride and joy.

When Donna had left, Sorrel and Alyse sat and looked at each other, Sorrel slumping despondently in her chair.

'If Pamela really intends to take the shop I'll have to visit the estate again soon,' Sorrel remarked.

'Marcus said there's no hurry. And he said he'll help you find somewhere else.'

'You seem to have a lot of faith in Marcus,' Sorrel remarked.

'Well,' Alyse was flustered, 'he's in a position to help. He must know lots of people.'

Sorrel stood up briskly. 'I don't think I want to bother about it for a while. Come on, let's have tea. I shan't want much to eat this evening. You should have seen Mrs Fry's chicken pie!' Chatting together, they locked the shop and went into the rooms at the back.

★ ★ ★

Two days later, it was Alyse's birthday and Sorrel had an idea for a treat for the occasion.

'How would you like to go to La Cenerentola to celebrate?' Sorrel asked.

'La Cenerentola? You mean that new place on the coast to Penmarron? Oh I'd love it!'

'What about asking Tony Redvers to come with us?' Sorrel suggested. 'We haven't seen him since that day Pamela had her accident.'

'Lovely idea. I like Tony. Why don't you phone him right now?'

That proved to be easier said than done, but after a few attempts, Sorrel managed to get hold of Tony. 'You're an elusive man!' she joked.

'We're very busy at the moment. I told you the place is closing, didn't I?'

'Yes. Any luck with finding a new job?'

'Not yet, but I have high hopes. Irons in the fire. You know.' He sounded evasive but Sorrel didn't press him.

She issued her invitation for dinner

that evening. 'It's Alyse's birthday. She'd love you to come.'

'I'd have loved to, but I have something on for this evening. Something connected with a new job, actually. Give her my love and best wishes, though, and tell her I'll take you both out soon to make up.'

Sorrel replaced the receiver despondently. Well, it would have to be just the two of them. She put on a cheerful expression and went to break the news to her cousin.

An hour later, as they were preparing for the evening out, Alyse was cheered by the arrival of a bouquet of pink roses. The accompanying card read, 'Sorry I can't come. Will these do instead? Happy birthday, Tony.'

'I'd rather have had Tony,' she commented, 'but these are beautiful.'

From what the girls had heard, La Cenerentola was rather smart. Sorrel gazed ruefully at her reflection in the bedroom mirror as she dressed and thought once again that an expedition to Truro to liven up her wardrobe would seem to be a necessity in the near future. She was wearing the deep blue silk which did duty as her best evening occasion dress. In fact, it had fulfilled that function for the past two years.

She made up her mind. She would go to Truro tomorrow if Donna could cover the shop. Cheered by her decision, she applied more lipstick and brushed her hair furiously.

Fifteen minutes later, they were on the coast road to Penmarron. Sorrel smiled across at her cousin. Alyse was wearing her new red dress and the jacket Sorrel had given her as a birthday present. Her face shone with happiness.

Sorrel told her of her plans for the next day.

'If Donna can come in to help you, I'm off to Truro,' she said. 'You're putting me to shame with your glamorous outfits. It's time I bought some new clothes myself.'

La Cenerentola was a long, low building, built perilously near the edge of the cliff. It was ablaze with lights as Sorrel swung into the carpark and parked near the restaurant entrance.

'If it rains later, we don't want a long walk to the car,' she pointed out as they got out.

Sea breezes swept across the carpark and they clutched their jackets round them against the chill and hurried to reach the warmth of the restaurant.

'Shall we have a drink first or go straight to our table?' Sorrel wondered.

'Let's eat,' said Alyse at once. 'I'm too hungry to wait and something smells wonderful!'

A waiter conducted them to their table and handed them leather-bound menus which offered an extensive selection of dishes, Italian and English.

'I'm having Italian,' Sorrel decided. 'It seems a shame to come to an Italian restaurant and eat English food.'

Alyse agreed. After much humming and hawing, they finally decided on their meals, placed their order with the very patient waiter who seemed faintly amused by their indecision, and then looked around their surroundings with interest.

The ceiling was low and hung with rows of twisted artificial vines to give the impression of an open-air Mediterranean restaurant. Bunches of grapes dangled from the vines and tiny lights glowed softly behind the leaves. White marble statues gleamed in the shadows at the sides of the room and small fountains tinkled in the centre.

'It certainly isn't Cornish,' Sorrel said with a laugh, as the waiter arrived with their starters. They tucked in with relish.

'This is delicious,' sighed Alyse after her first mouthful. 'I wonder if I could make it? There's cream and mushrooms — oh, and olives . . . '

'I remember my first visit to Italy,' Sorrel remarked. 'The waiter brought a huge bowl of pasta to the table and, thinking it was the main course, I asked for a large plateful. I thought he looked startled. I soon discovered why! The pasta was followed by four more courses. I could hardly move at the end of it all!'

Alyse laughed, then mused, 'I should love to visit Italy. My only holiday abroad was on a school trip to France. More work than play.'

Sorrel looked thoughtful. 'Maybe we could manage a short break in a few months' time?'

Alyse shook her head. 'Forget holidays. We'll have enough to do moving the shop,' she said decidedly, then added, 'But we don't want to think about *that* this evening.'

The waiter arrived with two plates of grilled lamb, fragrantly seasoned with herbs.

'It smells too delicious to eat,' said Alyse. 'Can you remember what it was called?'

'Lamb is *agnello* . . . ' Sorrel suggested.

'*Agnello alla griglia,*' the waiter told

them, returning to their table with a bottle of wine. 'Frascati,' he pointed to the label. 'Very nice. From Roma.'

The girls settled down to enjoy their meal.

'Thank you so much for thinking of this,' said Alyse. 'I *am* enjoying myself.' She lifted her glass to her lips and as she did so, looked across the room to the doorway. Her hand froze mid-movement. 'Sorrel! Look who's just come in!' she hissed.

Sorrel followed the direction of her glance to see that Tony Redvers had just entered the restaurant. With him was a tall, slim girl whose auburn hair shone in the lamp light.

'Pamela Barrington!' Sorrel exclaimed. 'So *she's* the something he had on this evening. But he said it was something connected with a new job.'

They watched as Pamela and Tony strolled the length of the room, his hand tucked beneath her elbow, she speaking confidingly to him.

'They seem very friendly,' observed

Alyse. 'This must have developed since the accident. He appeared very concerned about her when she fell.'

Sorrel raised her eyebrows but made no comment. She was thinking.

'A new job,' she mused. 'What if Pamela has asked him to help her set up the wine bar, even become the manager?'

'Then I suppose this could be called a business meeting,' giggled Alyse. 'But he's not being very fair to you. You're his friend.'

'*Only* a friend, though.' Sorrel placed her knife and fork carefully on her plate. 'Pamela could become much more. Thank goodness they can't see us. But don't let's talk about them. More wine?'

'You'd better not have any more. You're driving, remember, and we don't want to go over the cliff! I said we should have got a taxi.' With a rueful smile Alyse pushed a bottle of sparkling mineral water towards her cousin. 'Drink this and pretend it's champagne!'

Sorrel made a face but poured herself a glass of water, and they went on to discuss her shopping trip next day and what she should buy.

Bowls of creamy panna cotta with a delicious mixture of berries came next, and to finish they sipped rich Italian coffee.

Finally Alyse sat back in her seat with a sigh of satisfaction.

'That was absolutely wonderful. How can I possibly match it tomorrow night? But I shan't try. We'll have baked beans on toast,' she said gaily.

'Look — the dance floor,' Sorrel muttered, touching her arm. On the minuscule dance floor, one couple was circling slowly, intent only on each other. Pamela and Tony.

'Well, at least we'll be able to leave without them seeing us,' Sorrel commented and nodded to the waiter to bring their bill.

'It's lucky the dance floor is nowhere near the main door,' said Alyse as they slipped on their jackets and threaded their way across the room.

Outside they both breathed audible sighs.

'Mr Tony Redvers can certainly take us out when he's free.' Sorrel took the car keys from her bag. 'He owes us that!'

New Horizons

It was great to be driving out of St Towan early the next morning, the open window letting in gusts of fresh, salty air.

She breathed deeply and smiled to herself, feeling like a truant from school. Donna and Alyse would manage the shop for a few hours. She meant to enjoy herself and forget business for once.

Alyse had given her a pep talk over breakfast.

'No more black. You wear black every day. Buy something bright.'

'I don't feel right in bright clothes,' Sorrel had protested.

'Surprise yourself! Surprise us all!'

Now, leaving the country road and joining the main road to Truro, Sorrel made a mental list of what she hoped to buy. She lived in trousers at the moment, so she would look for boots and a couple of skirts. Then perhaps a jacket or two, jumpers and a dress for evenings. It was so long since she'd bought any new clothes. She had always been careful with money, hating extravagance, but she knew that good quality was an investment. She hummed to herself as she joined a queue of traffic approaching the city.

The carparks were filling rapidly. She headed towards the cathedral to the place where she usually parked and found a space. As she switched off the ignition she took a deep breath. Now for the hunt that would change her image.

Startled at the thought, she met her gaze in the vanity mirror on the sun visor. Change her image? For whom? Marcus — or Carl?

Resolutely she climbed out and locked the door. She was buying clothes for herself! She would bear that in mind when she chose them, she scolded herself as she walked away from the car and into the cobbled streets around the cathedral.

Many of the shops were branches of retail chains. She studied the models in the windows critically. Many of the clothes were aimed at girls much younger than herself. She didn't want to look silly. Next came a large shoe shop and she ducked in there for a leisurely browse round.

Half an hour later, she emerged swinging a bag containing tan knee-high boots and a pair of pewter-coloured high-heeled shoes.

'Suitable for evenings or dressy day wear,' the assistant had advised.

Well, she'd made a start. By the time another hour had passed she had two skirts and jackets; one jacket to match the conker brown skirt, the other a general purpose red corduroy.

Well satisfied, she took her purchases back to her car then looked around for a coffee shop. Rest and refreshment, she thought to herself, that's what I need now.

She sat in the window of the café with a mug of hot coffee and watched the passing crowds. Across the road, a familiar face emerged from the throng, a man with dark, wavy hair, turning into a photographic shop. Carl!

Her heartbeat quickened. What was he doing here? Then, as he reemerged, she decided that it wasn't Carl after all. She poured another cup from the cafetiére, added cream and stirred it absently.

Why had she felt so excited when she had thought it was Carl?

She sipped the coffee and told herself that she wasn't excited, just surprised. Carl was still in Germany, she supposed. And if he was back in England, why hadn't he contacted her as he'd promised?

She finished her coffee. She must forget Carl; she had shopping to do! Evening wear next, she decided.

Truro was full of tiny alleyways lined with speciality shops — jewellers, craft shops and clothes boutiques. Sorrel made for one where she knew of two interesting boutiques. The owner of the first was an old friend.

Sorrel studied the window. Pride of place was given to a tiered dress in different shades of pink. Accessories scattered artlessly around — scarves, necklaces and bracelets — were also pink. She gave a little grimace. She couldn't imagine herself in pink!

A bell tinkled as she entered the shop and Marian, the owner, came to greet her with a pleased smile.

'Sorrel! I haven't seen you for months. How are you? How's the shop?'

'We're both well.' She didn't want to discuss the bombshell Marcus had dropped. There was time enough for that when she found another shop.

'Are you playing truant?'

'I suppose I am! I've left Alyse and Donna in charge. I desperately need to update my wardrobe. Is pink the colour for this season?' She gestured unhappily towards the window.

'One of them. That's a particularly eye-catching dress so we decided to make a feature of it.'

Sorrel grimaced. 'But pink! I can't wear that!'

'Why not? Too girly?' Marian made a face at her.

'Probably. I'm happier in a stronger colour.'

Marian went to a rack and drew out a dress in a soft willow green. 'I don't suppose you'd call it a stronger colour, but it's quite lovely, don't you think? And it would suit you.'

Sorrel studied it in silence. The colour *was* lovely, she agreed. But was it too soft for her? She'd always seen herself as strong and wearing strong colours.

'Try it on,' urged Marian. 'Meanwhile I'll find something else in case you don't like it.'

Five minutes later Sorrel emerged from the changing room wearing the green dress and a pleased expression.

'I love it! It seems to do something

for me, I don't know what.'

'It compliments your hair and brings out the greeny shades in your eyes,' said Marian. 'I'd selected these two,' she indicated a blue, and a red sparkly dress, still on their hangers, 'but the green is perfect.'

'I've just bought pewter-coloured shoes,' said Sorrel. 'Would they go, d'you think?'

She slipped them on and both girls considered her reflection in the long mirror. Sorrel met Marian's gaze and they exchanged a smile of agreement. Perfect.

'I'll take it,' she said.

'Are you going somewhere special?' asked Marian through the curtain as Sorrel changed back into her own clothes.

Sorrel paused. That was the sad thing. She wasn't going anywhere special.

'Not yet,' she called cheerfully. 'But you never know!'

★ ★ ★

On her way back to the car, she popped into two more shops and added two jumpers and a denim skirt to her collection.

Humming softly with satisfaction, she crossed the cobbled area in front of the cathedral and turned on to the path through the garden at the side of the huge building which dominated the centre of the city.

She put her purchases into the boot of her car and locked it. All done, painlessly and satisfactorily, she thought. She consulted her watch. One-fifteen — time to head back.

She glanced towards the cathedral. Ten minutes would make little difference. Whenever she came to the city, she tried to find time for ten minutes' reflection in the peaceful atmosphere of the huge church.

She pushed open the door and entered. A few other visitors, obviously tourists, wandered around clutching guide books. A priest arranging leaflets on a table smiled a welcome.

She walked down the aisle towards the high altar, behind which was a spectacular reredos, lit from below so that its elaborate Biblical carvings stood out. It never failed to overwhelm her as she gazed at it.

In a seat a few rows from the front sat the man she had seen coming out of the camera shop, the man who looked like Carl. He was engrossed in contemplation of the huge altar screen.

As she drew level with him, he turned and caught her eye and she halted in surprise. It *was* Carl! He beckoned to her and she slid along the row and joined him.

'Isn't the screen amazing?' he whispered. 'I've never seen anything like it.'

'What are you doing here?' she whispered back.

'Enjoying the cathedral. Oh, I see, you mean what am I doing in England? I got back last night. I telephoned your shop this morning and they said you were in Truro. So I came to find you.'

'How did you know I would come to the cathedral?'

'I just knew.' He slid his hand across the bench between them and squeezed her fingers.

Confused, she stood up.

'Come and see the stained glass windows. Some people consider them the best Victorian glass windows in the country.'

'I've seen them.' He stood too, and together they moved down the aisle to the refectory. Now they could talk normally.

'Have you had lunch?' he asked.

'No, I was just going home.'

'Will you have something with me or do you have to go now?'

They agreed on coffee and a sandwich and were soon settled at a table for two in a window overlooking the garden.

'The funeral . . . ' she began, not quite knowing how to phrase her question.

He understood. 'It went well. The

142

church was full. Uncle Ernst would have been surprised at how many people remembered him.'

'I'm glad.' She looked out at the garden, remembering her old friend with sadness.

'Alyse said you were shopping for new clothes.' Carl's voice was bright, seeking to lighten the atmosphere.

'Mm. Not something I do very often.'

'You always look very nice to me.'

'But dark!' She acknowledged with a laugh. 'Alyse told me I must buy some brighter colours. So I have bought some very colourful clothes. All I need now is somewhere to go.' She spoke without thinking and instantly regretted the remark. Carl would think she was angling for a date.

She coloured up with embarrassment but Carl pretended not to notice and concentrated on his sandwich.

'Have you decided what you're going to do with the workshop?' she asked. 'Do you think you'll stay in England?'

'I have many ideas in my mind,' he

said solemnly. 'Now I must sort them out.'

'When you were in Bavaria, you didn't think you might stay there?'

'It is not far away by plane. I could live in both places,' he said with a smile.

She nodded. Obviously he wasn't prepared to share his plans.

He guessed her thoughts. 'As soon as I have decided what to do, I shall tell you,' he promised.

They chatted for a few minutes more then Sorrel picked up her bag and pushed back her chair.

'I really must be getting home. How are you travelling? Do you have a car?'

'Yes, a very nice hired one.' He laughed. 'Better than the old thing I drive at home.'

They walked together to the carpark.

'I also am parked here,' he said. 'Could I follow you out of the city? The roads are confusing.'

'You can try,' she said. 'I'll try not to lose you!'

However it was inevitable that with

the volume of traffic, he was soon lost to view. There's nothing I can do about it, she thought, staring anxiously in the mirror at the traffic weaving in and out behind her. I'll just have to hope he makes it back safely.

Switching on the radio for company, she settled down to complete the journey to St Towan. But the music went unheard as she contemplated the last two hours.

* * *

The telephone rang. It was Carl. 'Sorrel? You are back safely? Good. I had a few problems but I also am back safely. I have had an idea. Would you come and have supper with me this evening? I have something to show you.'

'I have a better idea,' she countered. 'You come and have supper with us. I've been out all day and I don't think I should abandon Alyse all evening as well. Don't worry — she's a very good

145

cook and you'll get an excellent supper.'

He laughed ruefully. 'Probably better than you would get here. I am not a good cook. Very well, I accept. Many thanks. At what time should I come?'

They agreed a time and Sorrel replaced the receiver.

'That was Carl,' she said, going into the kitchen. 'I've invited him to supper. You don't mind, do you?'

'Of course not. We'll get to know him better. What shall I cook? Wiener schnitzels?'

'I think he would prefer English cooking. How about one of your lovely cottage pies? With gooseberry tart and cream to follow. I'll top and tail the gooseberries.'

'No need, they're already prepared in the freezer. And I have some pastry ready to roll out, too, so the meal won't take long at all.'

'He says he has something to show me,' Sorrel mused. 'I wonder what it is?'

'A toy, of course. He wants to show

you that he's as good a toy maker as his uncle,' said Alyse.

'Oh, do you think so? That would be wonderful.' Sorrel hadn't thought of that. Then she remembered. 'If I still have a shop, of course,' she added gloomily.

Alyse shooed her out of the kitchen. 'That's enough of that! Go and lay out your new clothes. I want to see everything you've bought.'

When Carl arrived, he again produced a small bouquet of flowers for each girl and presented them with a bow, saying '*Grüss Gott.*'

'Carl, why do you say '*Grüss Gott*'? Good evening is *Guten Abend*, isn't it?' Sorrel queried.

'In German, it is *Guten Abend*. But I am Bavarian, and *Grüss Gott* is the traditional Bavarian greeting.'

' '*Grüss Gott*' — I must remember that when I visit Bavaria,' said Sorrel, and Carl looked up, his expression quizzical. 'I promised Ernst I would visit one day and see the castles,' she explained hastily.

Carl was carrying a large holdall on his shoulder. He lowered it to the ground and sat down, putting the bag carefully at the side of his chair.

'I have something interesting to show you after supper,' he said.

Sorrel looked at the bag speculatively. It was very large for one toy. Perhaps it was a collection of toys.

'Supper's ready,' called Alyse from the kitchen.

The meal was a great success. Alyse was happy to be cooking for an extra person, especially someone who was so appreciative. Occasionally she caught Sorrel's eye and gave a secret smile. She's showing me how well she's getting on with him, thought Sorrel. Does that mean she approves of him for me?

She observed Carl when he was engrossed in talking to Alyse. He wasn't as striking as Marcus, but he had an attraction of his own. His eyes crinkled as he smiled and his mouth was wide and generous. It would be easy to fall for him.

Alyse went into the kitchen to make the coffee and Sorrel and Carl cleared the table.

'I'm dying to see what's in that bag,' she said.

He placed a felt cloth on the table, then lifted the bag on to a stool next to his chair and began to take out small cardboard boxes.

'Come and sit down,' he said, 'and you shall see all.'

The girls joined him at the table and waited expectantly. He opened the first box and removed a tiny table, three inches across. The top was inlaid with minute squares of polished wood in different colours.

Alyse reached out a fingertip and touched the table. 'How perfect,' she breathed.

Next, he produced a little desk complete with leather top and opening drawers. He set a high-backed armchair behind the desk. Sorrel gazed at it without speaking.

Within ten minutes, the table was covered with exquisite examples of miniature furniture — chairs, beds, stools and tiny wooden utensils.

'You've made all these?' Sorrel was fascinated.

He nodded. 'These are not children's toys, these are collectors' pieces.'

'Not for doll's-houses?'

'Not children's doll's-houses. Adult collectors' doll's-houses: I make the houses too.'

'Do many people collect these things?' asked Alyse.

'In England and America, there must be thousands of collectors. And the hobby is becoming very popular on the Continent.'

Sorrel looked thoughtful. 'So you're not a toy maker like Ernst?'

'No. I'm sorry. I cannot supply your shop. But I have been thinking about this. Instead of the wooden toys my uncle made, why don't you specialise in miniature furniture and collectors' houses? There is an enormous range available, modern and historical.'

Sorrel was silent, thinking.

'You could interest the people here in the hobby,' he went on, 'and existing collectors in this part of Cornwall would be so pleased to have their own specialist shop. Then there are always the holiday visitors looking for a gift or a memento to take home with them.'

Sorrel picked up a miniature book-case and studied it, then a tiny wall clock.

'It tells the time,' said Carl. 'I have many different clocks which work perfectly.'

'And you would supply these things?'

'I and many other miniaturists.'

Alyse was watching Sorrel closely. Sorrel caught her eye and smiled. 'What do you think, Alyse?'

Alyse shook her head. 'I can't advise you. It's your business and your decision.'

'Would you be able to leave your

shop for a few days?' asked Carl.

Sorrel frowned. 'Why?'

'I have a suggestion that might help you make up your mind. Next week there will be held a huge exhibition of miniature work. I shall go. If you would permit, I could take you. There are thousands of pieces to look at and to buy.'

'And where is this exhibition?'

'Near Birmingham.'

'Birmingham! But that's hours away! It would take all day to get there.'

'That is why I asked if you could leave your shop for a few days. We could go up on Friday, stay the night, spend all day Saturday at the exhibition and travel back on Sunday.'

Alyse slid off her chair. 'I'll make some more coffee,' she said, and disappeared into the kitchen.

She doesn't want a part in this discussion, Sorrel thought.

She looked at Carl. He was replacing the tiny objects in the boxes, a little smile playing around his lips.

'We could have an enjoyable excursion,' he said.

She watched as he replaced the last box in his bag.

'When you have seen all the wonderful things at the exhibition, I'm sure you will be very keen,' he said.

'I don't know,' she replied slowly. 'It would be such a change. I've always sold children's toys.'

'Don't try to decide now. Wait until we've been to Birmingham.'

Alyse came in then with a tray of coffee. 'Could you manage without Sorrel for a few days?' he asked her.

'Don't rush us,' Sorrel put in quickly. 'I must think about it.'

'Sleep on it,' he said heartily, as if sure she would agree. 'Let me know tomorrow what you have decided. I am going anyway. I must make arrangements. And don't forget,' he gave her a sly grin, 'you wanted somewhere to wear your new clothes.'

He finished his coffee, stood up and picked up the bag of furniture, swinging it carefully on to his shoulder.

'My thanks again for a wonderful supper,' he said to Alyse, with one of his little bows.

Sorrel saw him to the door. He took her hand and kissed it. 'Until tomorrow.' Then, without a backward glance, he strode away.

Sorrel went slowly into the kitchen where Alyse was washing the coffee cups.

'Do you feel as if he's trying to rush me along?' she asked her.

Alyse began to wipe the cups. 'He *is* very charming, but there's something I don't quite trust. Perhaps he's *too* charming.'

Sorrel considered for a moment.

'*Could* you manage for a few days — with Donna, of course — if I went with him to the exhibition?'

'If you're thinking about taking up his suggestion, you *must* go to the exhibition. Of course Donna and I can manage.'

Sorrel placed the clean cups in the

cupboard. 'It would be fun to go somewhere totally different,' she conceded.

'And you could wear your new clothes,' Alyse pointed out. 'Think of it as a little holiday.'

Sorrel smiled at her. 'Let's sleep on it. I'll decide in the morning.'

'I think you've already decided,' said her cousin with an impish smile.

Can Carl Be Trusted?

Sorrel settled herself in the passenger seat of Carl's hired car while he put her luggage in the boot and locked it. Then he came to the front, slid behind the steering-wheel and fastened his seat-belt.

'Ready?' he asked, smiling across at her. 'Or do you want to change your mind?'

She made a face at him and leaned forward to wave goodbye to Alyse who, in her dressing-gown, was peeping round the front door.

A few seconds later, they were driving through the narrow, almost deserted streets of St Towan and out on to the main road. It was just past dawn.

'Is it too late to change my mind now?' she teased.

'Much too late! I have kidnapped you. We shan't stop until your inn on the moor.'

She nodded. 'Jamaica Inn on Bodmin Moor. We should be there by eight-thirty, in time for breakfast,' she explained.

The early morning mist drifted across the road as they drove. While Carl hummed quietly to himself, Sorrel opened a road map and studied the route.

'Goodness, we've got a long way to go!' she exclaimed.

'Good. We can really get to know each other. I think the journey will take about seven hours. At the end of that, there will be nothing I do not know about you.'

She laughed. 'That sounds ominous! Are you going to question me all the way?'

'No. We shall talk — like friends. And you will tell me all about yourself.'

'And what about you?'

'I shall tell you all about myself, too, of course.'

If they were going to work together, that would be a good idea, thought Sorrel. She stole a glance at her companion. He was staring through the window, all his concentration on the traffic which was beginning to build up. It wouldn't be a good idea to start a conversation until they reached a less congested road.

She looked at the dramatic landscape flanking the road. The softer country-side around the little villages had gone. Here it was brown and bare, open heathland and straggling muddy pools, with craggy tors in the distance. Bodmin Moor. The name had a dramatic feel to it, especially to someone from the coast.

The long road stretched ahead, busy even at this early hour. At her side, Carl relaxed.

'Now we just sit in the traffic and go,' he said. 'We are not in a hurry. Now, tell me why you have a toyshop.'

* * *

Thick mist had built up and swirled around the car. Through a gap, Sorrel

158

spotted the sign, Jamaica Inn.

'Turn here,' she said, directing him off the main road on to a side road which led directly to the inn. Carl turned in at the wide stone gateway and parked in the shelter of a wall.

'So this is your famous Jamaica Inn. It must have been very lonely in the days when there were no tourists.'

'It was a smugglers' inn. It needed to be remote.'

'I know about smugglers,' he said airily. ' 'Four and twenty ponies trotting through the dark, brandy for the parson, baccy for the clerk',' he quoted and Sorrel laughed.

'How on earth d'you know that?' she asked, amazed.

' 'Smugglers sailed their boats to France and returned with brandy and lace and tobacco. They hid it in caves and places like Jamaica Inn and then sold it to people who wanted to avoid paying the duty on such things,' ' he recited.

The penny dropped. 'Ernst's book,'

she said, remembering the book she had taken to the old toy maker in hospital. 'You've been reading that.'

He nodded. 'It was in his locker at the hospital. They gave it to me with his other belongings. I began to read it last night. It told me all about smugglers.'

She looked through the car window at the sprawling buildings.

'The inn would have been much smaller in the smugglers' days,' she said. 'It's been extended to form a large dining-room, but you can still get some idea of what it was like. Come on, I'm hungry.'

They entered the inn and were soon sitting in the large, dark dining-room with its red carpet and oak tables and chairs, tucking into substantial cooked breakfasts.

'I enjoy your English breakfasts,' said Carl, spearing a sausage. 'Much better than the croissants and coffee you get in France.'

'Look,' said Sorrel, pointing through the small-paned windows, 'the mist has cleared. We can see Brown Willy from here.'

'Brown Willy,' Carl repeated. 'What a strange name. What is it?'

'The hill over there. See?'

'But it is green, not brown.'

She shrugged. 'I know. Brown Willy is just the name. I don't know why. Would you like some more coffee?'

Carl pushed away his plate with a satisfied sigh. 'That was good. Yes, please, more coffee. Then we must be on our way.'

The journey up the centre of England was long and sometimes boring. The scenery, a blur of rich, undulating grassland and farms tucked into folds of small hills, changed after a few hours to the flatter countryside of the Midlands.

Her early start and the large breakfast at the inn made Sorrel feel sleepy and her eyes began to close. She wanted to stay awake to keep Carl company, but at last she slept.

The slight bump as the car stopped

nudged her awake. She opened her eyes, bewildered. Carl was grinning at her.

'Hello! Coffee stop. Are you coming or do you want to stay here and sleep?'

'I wasn't asleep,' she protested indignantly. 'I just had my eyes closed.'

He looked at his watch. 'Well, you kept them closed for two hours.'

Her eyes widened. 'Two hours! Oh my goodness! Where are we?'

'A service station near Bristol. There is not so far to go now, I think. Come on, a walk and some fresh air will do you good. You must be stiff. I know I am.'

Sorrel eased herself out of the car and stretched, glad of the fresh breeze on her cheeks.

A short walk around and a cup of tea refreshed them, and it wasn't more than thirty minutes before they were on their way again.

'You know all about me,' Sorrel said as they slid into the stream of motorway traffic. 'Tell me about *your* family.'

For a moment he looked confused. 'My family?'

'Yes. Have you any brothers and sisters? What does your father do?'

'Oh, I see. My father is dead. He was a wood carver like Uncle Ernst. My mother lives in the village where I was born. I have two sisters. They are married and live in Munchen — Munich.'

She would have liked to ask him if he had a girlfriend, but felt rather shy about it.

'Do you live at home with your mother?' she tried instead.

'No, I have my own house.'

He seemed unwilling to elaborate on any of his answers so she had to be satisfied.

She changed the subject to ask, 'Where are we staying? Is the hotel near the exhibition centre?'

'No. It is very busy there. I know a small hotel in a village ten miles from the exhibition area. I have stayed there before. You will like it.'

As they drove on in silence, Sorrel wondered idly how Alyse and Donna were managing. Probably very well, she thought. They were both sensible and knew exactly what to do.

She looked out of the window, wishing she was driving. She felt fidgety with nothing to do. But the car hire agreement didn't allow it.

The car began to veer to the left on to a slip road.

'We're leaving the motorway?' she asked.

'Yes. The village is this way.'

She was glad to leave the motorway with its noise and its incessant stream of cars and coaches and lorries. At the end of the slip road they turned into a country lane edged with houses standing in large gardens.

'You drive as confidently as if you were in your own country,' she said admiringly.

He shrugged. 'I have been here twice before and I have a good memory for directions.'

As last they reached the hotel. It wasn't large, but it was elegantly painted, its stonework white, its wood-work glossy black, and brightly-coloured hanging baskets added splashes of gaiety.

Carl led the way into the reception area where he gave his name to the pretty receptionist. She consulted her register.

'Number twenty-seven,' she said, taking a key from the board behind the desk and giving it to Carl.

There was a pause, and Sorrel looked at her questioningly. 'And my room?'

The girl looked at her in surprise, then at Carl. 'Oh, but — I'm sure a double room was reserved . . . ' she began.

With a quick glance at Sorrel, whose cheeks were flushing hotly, Carl put the key back on the desk. '*Nein*. There has been a mistake. We wanted single rooms.'

The receptionist looked like she might argue the point, and Sorrel looked at Carl suspiciously, but he kept his face averted from her.

With a faint shrug, the receptionist consulted her book again. 'I can offer you two single rooms on different floors,' she told him.

'That will be fine,' Sorrel agreed quickly and held out her hand for the key.

★ ★ ★

They climbed the stairs in silence. At the door of her room, Carl took her key from her to open her door for her, and placed her case just inside the room.

'I'll see you in the lounge in an hour,' he said, and strode off down the corridor towards the stairs.

Sorrel closed the door and looked about her. It was a pretty room, decorated in pink and white, but she didn't feel in the mood to admire the décor. What an embarrassing scene! What must the receptionist have thought? She was sure the girl didn't believe that there had been a mistake.

She wasn't sure she believed it herself.

She frowned. Perhaps Alyse was right, perhaps there was something not quite trustworthy about Carl . . .

An hour later, showered, changed and freshly made-up, she felt refreshed and more inclined to give Carl the benefit of the doubt. After all, so far he had always been a perfect gentleman.

She found him sitting in the colourful, chintzy lounge downstairs, with a tray of tea on the table in front of him. He jumped to his feet with a welcoming smile as she came in.

So he's going to forget the incident, she thought. Very well, so shall I.

They drank their tea looking out at the flower-filled garden.

'I've booked dinner here for tonight,' he said. 'Will that suit you or would you prefer to go out?'

'No more car journeys today,' she protested with a laugh. 'Dinner here will be fine.'

'We have a few hours to pass till then. Would you like to go for a walk? The village is very pretty,' he coaxed.

'Just a short one, then I'd like to go to my room and read. I hardly ever get the chance to just sit around and read, so it'll be a real treat.'

'Come on then. But first,' he put a hand on her arm, his expression concerned, 'I must apologise about the rooms. The hotel made a mistake. Perhaps the telephone and my accent . . .'

'Of course. Forget it. I have. And my room is delightful.' She turned and walked towards the door. 'Let's go before the sun goes in and it gets cold.'

The village had several black-and-white houses, a few shops and a small bulrush-edged duck pond. Sorrel found its softness a change from the granite hardness of her Cornish home town.

In half an hour, their tour was complete.

'What shall you do now?' she asked, as they prepared to part in the foyer of the hotel.

'I shall go for a longer walk. At home, I take long walks over the mountain paths. Sometimes I am out all day. I shall see you at dinner. Enjoy your read.'

In her bedroom, Sorrel took two books from her case, plumped up the pillows and made herself comfortable on the bed. But it was hard to concentrate on reading. She felt unsettled. What was she doing here, miles from home and her shop, with someone she barely knew? Was it an adventure, or was she being silly?

She wondered whether to telephone Alyse. But it might seem as if she was checking up when she had nothing of interest to report herself. Tomorrow night would be better. She turned to her book again . . .

An hour later, her eyes fluttered open. Her gaze travelled round the room, flustered for a moment by its strangeness. Of course, she was in the hotel with Carl.

She looked at the book she was still holding. The same page! She must have fallen asleep immediately. She glanced at her watch. Thank goodness, there was still plenty of time to get ready for dinner.

Dinner was beautifully cooked. She chose melon basket, followed by roast lamb with baby new potatoes and sweet minted peas.

'And now for something creamy,' said Carl. 'At home we have wonderful cream. I cannot resist it.'

'Well, I can,' she said firmly. 'Just coffee, please.'

His face fell. 'But then if I have anything else, you will think I am very greedy.'

'Not at all! You have what you like.' Then she relented. 'Oh, all right, I'll have an apricot sorbet just to keep you company.'

He gave her his charming smile. 'You are a very kind girl.'

'Did you have a good walk?' she asked once they had placed their order.

'Excellent,' he said with a sigh of contentment. 'Spending so long in that car had twisted me up. Now I am stretched out.'

'I was stretched out too,' she admitted. 'I fell asleep on the bed! So much for reading a chapter of my book!'

They took their coffee into the lounge and settled by the log fire. They had the room to themselves.

'You look very charming this evening,' he said.

Sorrel looked down at her fluid grey wool skirt and aqua-coloured top. If she looked charming in this old outfit, why had she bothered to buy new clothes? But she smiled her thanks for the compliment.

Alyse had tried to persuade her to take her new green dress, but she had declined.

'Are you saving it for a special occasion?' her cousin had teased.

'A more important occasion than this, at least,' she had protested. Perhaps an occasion with Marcus?

'Do we have an early start again tomorrow?' she asked now.

'No. The exhibition opens at ten so we have plenty of time for breakfast.

We're not far away.'

They sat for a while chatting about Ernst and Bavaria and their own different lives. Sorrel mentioned nothing about Pamela's ultimatum. There was time enough for that when she had made a decision about the toys.

★　★　★

After a good breakfast the next morning, they set out for the National Exhibition Centre near Birmingham. The road was busy but well signposted and before long they were entering the system of roads and islands and roundabouts that made up the exhibition complex. Huge halls made of red and blue girders and acres of glass reared up on all sides.

They were waved on by efficient yellow-jacketed stewards and soon found themselves parked in one of the numerous carparks. Carl locked the car and they followed the crowds to the appropriate hall.

Sorrel was relieved to find that her new boots were already comfortable. She had decided to wear the new conker brown skirt as a change from trousers, while her newly-washed hair swung loose on her shoulders, another change from its usual efficient pony-tail. Carl had looked at her approvingly when she appeared for breakfast and she had been glad she'd made the effort.

Miniatura said a sign above the entrance to their hall. Carl presented the tickets and they entered.

Sorrel had never been in such a large enclosed space. It was the size of an aeroplane hangar and filled with lights and display stands and the buzz of conversation and activity.

Carl opened a catalogue. 'Apparently there are two hundred stands,' he informed her.

She looked at him in dismay. 'Two hundred? Where do we start?'

'We need a plan,' he decided. 'We'll go all round the outside first, then see what is in the centre.'

Sorrel looked about in amazement. 'So many people! Where have they all come from?'

'This is an international fair,' he explained. 'Exhibitors come from all over Europe, and many from America. I told you, it is a growing hobby. You must think seriously about getting involved.'

The first stand featured buildings — large Tudor houses, mills with turning water wheels, village pubs and elegant town houses with basements and, sometimes, conservatories at the side. Sorrel was amazed at an Edwardian villa which stood taller than her and contained eighteen or twenty rooms.

They moved on to a display of exquisitely-costumed figures, mostly in historical fashion.

'How can they get such perfect detail into a figure only five or six inches tall?' she marvelled, admiring the tiny features and the ruffles, frills and lace of the clothes.

A hat stand came next: tiny cloches for the 1920s, sweeping feathered creations for an earlier time and many styles for historical figures.

By now she was thoroughly enjoying herself and she hurried Carl from display to display. Lighting: chandeliers and table lamps. Food: jellies, elaborate cakes, joints of meat and bowls of eggs. Fruit and vegetables in glistening colours, and fabrics, tiny rolls of silks and cottons, all their patterns scaled down to miniature.

They finished their circuit of the hall and Carl turned to her. 'I don't know about you, but I could do with a coffee.'

The restaurant was almost full, but they managed to find a table.

'This is the limited ticket day,' he said, looking around. 'Goodness knows how they manage tomorrow when they let everyone in!'

He looked quizzically across the table at Sorrel. 'Well?'

She gazed back blankly. 'Well what?'

'Have you made a decision? You're

obviously interested.'

'Who wouldn't be? It's fascinating! I've never seen such beautiful craft work.' She took another sip of her coffee. 'But I can't decide just like that. I need time to consider.'

'Of course you do. Come on — drink up, we have the centre stands to see next.'

As they made their way to the centre aisle, Sorrel heard Carl talking behind her — but she couldn't understand what he was saying. Turning, she saw that he had halted and was vigorously shaking the hand of a dark, bearded man whose delighted smile matched his.

Suddenly the flood of strange language — she realised it must be German — ceased and they both looked at her.

'I'm sorry.' Carl drew her forward. 'Sorrel, this is a good friend of mine, Heini Flessa. Heini, my friend, Sorrel Basset.'

Heini gave her an admiring glance as

he took her hand and carried it to his lips. Another charmer, she thought.

'Forgive us if we speak German,' Carl said to her with an apologetic smile. 'It is easier to explain.'

Explain what, she wondered.

While they chatted, she examined the objects in Heini's display. He special-ised in furniture and decorations for tiny inns. She picked up a little wooden settle with intricate carving on the back, then a set of tables and stools, all beautifully decorated.

Carl turned back to her. 'I have explained to Heini that you are thinking of changing from toys to miniatures.'

'Is a good idea,' said Heini. 'But could you not do both?'

Sorrel and Carl looked blankly at each other.

'Why didn't we think of that?' she exclaimed with a laugh. 'It wouldn't be as radical as a complete change of stock.'

Customers arrived at the stand and they shook hands with the big German and moved on.

'I can't help thinking it's amazing that such a big man can carve such lovely tiny things,' said Sorrel.

'He is a craftsman,' Carl replied simply.

By the time they had visited the rest of the stands, Sorrel's mind was a jumble of impressions. They had seen colourful stained glass windows; garden plants and furniture; oil and water-colour paintings; wrought iron lamps and railings, and tiny books, beautifully illustrated, whose texts could be read easily with the aid of a magnifying glass.

'I don't think I can take in any more,' she sighed.

'We'll have a cup of tea and something to eat,' said Carl, 'then we can sit down for a while.'

* * *

'Did you know that Heini would be here?' she asked as she finished a chicken sandwich and poured more tea for them both.

He nodded. 'He comes most years, so

I had a good idea that he would be here.'

'Why don't you have a stand yourself and sell your furniture?'

'There is a waiting list for stands. I will be notified when I can do that. While I am waiting, I work hard to increase my stock.'

Sorrel reached into the MINIA-TURA carrier bag she had been given when they arrived and pulled out a pile of advertising leaflets.

'I collected these from the stands,' she said. 'They'll remind me of the things I have seen. I have enjoyed today,' she went on enthusiastically. 'Even if I decide not to change my shop, I'll know so much more about an interesting hobby.'

'I hope you decide in favour of it, though. I want us to work together.' He reached across the table and took her hand, gazing at her intently. 'You would like that, wouldn't you?'

She allowed the pressure of his fingers for a few minutes, then gently withdrew her hand.

'You're rushing me again, Carl. I must have time to think. I don't want to make the wrong decision.'

'We'll come to the Spring show,' he said, as if she hadn't spoken, 'and you can register for the trade show. That's where businesses go . . . '

'Please, Carl, slow down,' she said. 'Come along, let's have another look round.'

By four o'clock, even Sorrel had had enough.

'I can't take in any more!' she protested. 'Can we go back to the hotel now, please?'

He smiled, put an arm round her shoulders and hugged her.

'Of course, but you have enjoyed today, haven't you?'

'It's been lovely,' she agreed warmly. 'Thank you so much for suggesting it.'

They left the hall and headed to the carpark. Sorrel was glad to be out in the fresh air after the warmth indoors.

Her mind was such a whirl of

impressions that she spoke little on the journey to the hotel and they were turning into the drive before she realised they were back.

'I need a shower and a rest,' she said as they climbed the stairs to their rooms. 'I'm so tired. I don't suppose even you'll want a walk after today.'

'I have some telephone calls to make,' he said. 'I shall see you at dinner. And, Sorrel . . . ' She turned to look and him. 'Thank you for coming with me. It was so nice to have a companion.' She made no protest when he lightly kissed her cheek.

She closed the door of her room, pulled off her boots and rolled on to the bed. Dear Carl, he had behaved impeccably today. Had she misjudged him over the room booking?

She lay on her back and gazed at the ceiling. There was so much to think about, but she felt too tired to think. She'd better have a shower before she fell asleep. But first she would phone Alyse.

Alyse answered immediately and her voice squeaked with excitement.

'Oh, Sorrel, I've been dying for you to phone! I've got such fabulous news!'

'News? What's happened?'

'I ought to wait until you get back but I'm too excited. Marcus came to see me last night. He said he would keep me company for an hour since you were away.'

Sorrel felt herself go cold. Marcus, and exciting news. Please, no . . .

'Guess what he wants to do?' Alyse's voice came again.

Marry you, thought Sorrel. It has to be that. I've lost him.

'He wants to send me to America for the operation.'

'I . . . ' Sorrel couldn't speak for overwhelming surprise and relief.

'Did you hear what I said?' Alyse pressed. 'He wants to send me to America for the operation.'

'But why? I mean, it's very kind, but why should he suggest it?'

'Because he *is* kind and thoughtful.

He took a long time to persuade me — it didn't seem right somehow — but he insists he can afford it. And he says we're friends — ' her voice suddenly sounded shy ' — and friends help each other, and he wants to help me.'

When they had finished talking, Sorrel sat and stared into space. Whatever Alyse said about friendship, it didn't make sense. Why should Marcus spend so much money on her? He must want something in return. And if that something was marriage . . . Oh, Marcus. I don't want Carl or anybody else. I love you.

Suddenly her eyes were full of tears.

A Proposal...

The journey home was uneventful. Carl wanted to talk about the exhibition, but Sorrel wanted to think about Alyse's news, and after her third lapse into a long silence, he stopped trying to engage her in conversation, thinking that perhaps she was tired.

Sorrel leaned her head against the back of the seat and closed her eyes, but she didn't sleep. She was willing the journey to be over. She was desperate to see Alyse. She would know by the younger girl's demeanour what had really passed between her and Marcus.

For most of the journey, it rained heavily, and Sorrel felt that the rainsoaked landscape matched her mood. Her euphoria of the day before had evaporated, leaving her prey to miserable thoughts.

Why would Marcus offer to help

Alyse unless he was in love with her?

At long last, they descended the hill into St Towan. The rain had stopped and the narrow streets were full of visitors. Carl drove carefully down the main street and round the church at the bottom to stop outside Sorrel's shop. Alyse, who had been watching for the car, rushed out.

'Sorrel! I'm so glad you're back. I've really missed you.'

They hugged affectionately, then Sorrel turned to take her bag and coat from the car. Carl lifted her case from the boot and carried it into the house for her.

'Stay for tea,' begged Alyse. 'I want to hear all about your trip.'

'Thank you, but no.' Carl gave her one of his little bows. 'Sorrel has had enough of me, I'm sure.' He smiled to take the sting out of this remark. 'She will tell you about our trip and I will come again tomorrow if I may.'

Then he was gone. Sorrel carried her case upstairs and when she came down,

Alyse had laid the little table by the fire and was pouring tea.

'Have you enjoyed yourself? Are you going to do as Carl suggests and change the shop? What sort of things did you see?'

'I'll tell you all about it later. Right now I want to hear about you and Marcus.'

Alyse's face glowed. 'He's a wonderful friend. He called in on Friday night and was concerned about my hip. Oh, I hadn't meant to say that.' She looked stricken.

'You were in pain! Alyse, I'm so sorry. Was it bad? I shouldn't have gone away and left you.'

'Please, don't be silly. I managed. I had Donna. It was just a bad day. You know how I get them sometimes.'

'Yes, but if I hadn't gone away . . .'

Alyse glared at her. 'If you say any more, I shan't tell you about Marcus!' she threatened.

Sorrel dropped her eyes. 'Sorry — I'm fussing. Go on then, tell me about Marcus.'

'As I said, he was concerned. We talked. He asked me about the operation, I told him, and after an hour or so, he went away. But he came back later. He'd spent the time on his computer, verifying what I'd said and contacting the American hospital. He told me he has arranged for me to have the operation next month.'

'Next month!'

'Yes.' Alyse's eyes were shining. 'He has a friend who's over here just now but she's returning to America then, and I'm to travel with her and stay in her home.'

'Goodness, he worked fast! What about the cost?'

'He said he wouldn't discuss that. I was his friend and in pain, that was all that mattered. He could afford it and insisted on helping.'

'Well!' Sorrel could think of nothing to say. Marcus's fortune must have improved if he could give thousands away like this. And he had known Alyse for such a short time. Could you want to do so much for someone after such a short friendship — *only* out of friendship?

'I told him I insisted on paying him back one day, but he just said, 'We'll see,' and changed the subject.'

'I'm pleased for you,' said Sorrel. 'I would have given anything to be able to help you myself.'

'You *have* helped me — enormously.' Alyse put her arms around her and laid her cheek against hers. 'You've given me a home and a new life. And you've looked after me. I'll always be grateful.'

Sorrel returned her hug warmly. 'You're welcome. Our lives seem to be changing rapidly, don't they?' she observed. 'You're going away, Ernst has died, Carl has appeared, my shop will change . . . '

'And you would like to say that Marcus has changed.' Alyse smiled wickedly. 'But you like to think bad things of him, don't you?'

Do I? thought Sorrel. Am I so unfair?

'There's so much to do before I go,'

chattered Alyse. 'What a good thing I've just had a shopping spree. But I shall need new nightdresses and dressing-gowns for the hospital.'

'We'll go shopping next week,' Sorrel promised. 'And I insist on buying you what you need.' She waved away the other girl's protests. 'When will you meet his American friend?'

'She was actually a friend of his mother's,' said Alyse. 'I don't know when I'll meet her. He said he'll be in touch with more details. Now, tell me all about your trip. How did you get on with Carl?'

Sorrel told her everything, even about the mix-up with the hotel rooms.

'Hmm. Do you think it was a genuine mistake?' asked Alyse, frowning doubt-fully.

Sorrel shrugged. 'I'm going to give him the benefit of the doubt. He behaved impeccably the rest of the time.'

'Mm.' Alyse looked unconvinced, and Sorrel leapt to his defence.

'I know you said there's something you don't trust about him, but I think you might be mistaken.'

'I hope so, for your sake.'

'Not for my sake,' Sorrel said hastily. 'Like you and Marcus, we're just friends.'

She watched Alyse carefully as she said this, but Alyse just smiled at her, warmly and innocently, and said, 'Well, that's all right then.'

They chatted for the rest of the evening, until Sorrel decided she needed an early night. The travelling and the excitement of the weekend had tired her out.

'And it's back to work tomorrow,' she said, as she climbed the stairs.

* * *

Marcus appeared as she was closing up the shop the following afternoon.

'Did you have a good trip?' he asked, and Sorrel sensed a coolness in his tone. Perhaps he resented her going away with Carl. But what business was it of his? He had shown no particular interest in her; in fact, his interest appeared to be in Alyse.

'Is Alyse in?' he asked without waiting for her reply.

'Yes. Go on in.' She nodded towards the back of the shop. But as he moved towards the door, she said awkwardly, 'It's very good of you to help her.'

He looked embarrassed. 'Not at all. I'm fond of her, and she seems to be in a lot of pain sometimes.'

So that was the reason for the coolness. He thought Sorrel had gone off for a weekend with Carl, leaving her cousin in pain and doing her best to run the business.

She opened her mouth to say something, then closed it again and turned away to tidy up the Lego bricks. She wouldn't have a pointless argument with him.

She remained in the shop, finding odd jobs to do, until he had finished with Alyse. She didn't want to intrude and Alyse would tell her all about it later on.

Eventually Marcus came through on his own.

'I'm afraid I have to give you this.' He reached into an inside pocket of his jacket and drew out an envelope, his manner apologetic.

Sorrel slid out the letter it contained and scanned it briefly. So it was final. The lease was not to be renewed.

'So Pamela really intends to take my shop,' she said flatly.

Marcus couldn't meet her eyes. 'I'm sorry. I've argued with her, but this is exactly the place she wants — opposite the sea and . . . '

'I know. You've already told me.'

'I'll help you find somewhere else,' he insisted.

She bit her lip and walked to the window, looking out at the waves and the rocks and the seabirds; they were an important part of what the location meant to her.

'Perhaps I won't stay in St Towan,'

she said softly, almost to herself.

'You're thinking of leaving?' he asked, an undercurrent of something unreadable in his voice.

She shrugged. 'I could give up the business and go to my family in Australia. Once Alyse is better she'll probably move away — get a job. If I lose my shop . . .'

He crossed the room and stood behind her, his hands on her shoulders. 'Sorrel, let me help.'

It would have been so easy to relax, to lean against him and feel his arms close around her. It was so tempting . . . Instead, she moved away from him, her shoulders rigid.

'You're helping Alyse. That's enough.'

'Perhaps your new friend has some ideas,' he suggested bitterly. 'Perhaps you'd prefer to accept help from him.'

As if on cue, Carl passed the window at that moment, heading for the front door.

Marcus gave her a furious look. 'I'll go out this way,' he said, going to the shop door. 'I don't think Herr Schumann and I have anything to say to each other.'

'Suit yourself,' she said, unlocking the door for him.

Sorrel led Carl into the sitting-room where Alyse was curled up in an armchair with an excited look of anticipation on her face.

'Marcus has brought me all the details,' she began at once. Then she caught sight of Carl behind Sorrel. 'Carl, come in and hear my news!'

Sorrel tried to forget her fury with Marcus and share in Alyse's happiness.

Mrs Goldman, the American friend, was returning to her home in Dallas after a few months in Europe. She lived alone and liked the idea of having Alyse with her as company. Alyse would live in her house, before and after the operation.

'Marcus is collecting me on Sunday to meet Mrs Goldman at her house,' said Alyse. 'I hope she likes me or she might change her mind!'

'No-one could help liking you, *Fräulein* Alyse,' said Carl and Alyse beamed at him.

'I'm so lucky, I never imagined I would be able to have the operation!' she bubbled.

Carl looked inquiringly at Sorrel.

'Marcus Barrington has offered to pay for Alyse to go to America and have the operation that will repair her hip,' she explained briefly.

Carl looked at the younger girl's shining face. 'I am very glad for you. How lucky to have such a generous friend. When do you go?'

'In about four weeks.' Alyse stood up. 'I think I'll go to my room for a bit. It's silly, I know, but I feel so happy I think I might cry and I don't want to embarrass you.'

'It's like a miracle for her,' Sorrel explained as the door closed behind Alyse. 'She has been saving up for the operation but . . .'

'Forgive me, but will it not be very expensive?'

195

'Exactly.'

'So Herr Barrington must be very fond of Alyse. Perhaps he is in love with her?'

Sorrel turned away, unable to trust herself to speak for the moment. Then she looked at Carl.

'Have you eaten? I could rustle up something . . . '

'Let's go out,' Carl said. 'I'm sure you don't want to cook. Oh, but I forgot Alyse. Perhaps she would like to come with us.'

Sorrel went to ask but was soon back. 'She doesn't feel like eating. She's too excited!'

'Then we go alone,' said Carl happily, and Sorrel knew it was what he had wanted all along.

As they left, she popped the letter from Marcus into her handbag. It would be good to discuss it with someone who wasn't involved.

'On one of my walks, I spotted a new restaurant at the end of the harbour,' he told her. 'I think it was called The

Albatross. We shall go there.'

'The Albatross?' she exclaimed. 'Are you sure? I've heard it's very expensive. There are lots of others we could go to.'

'We shall go to The Albatross,' he insisted. 'Come.'

He held open the door and Sorrel went past him into the street without another word. She had wanted to visit The Albatross ever since it opened at the beginning of the season. Now that her small protest had been brushed aside, she would enjoy herself.

Carl tucked her hand under his arm and together they strolled along the road skirting the harbour. At the end of the harbour wall, a beacon turned slowly, its beam of light crossing the sea, then the cliffs, then the harbour, then back out to sea. A few seagulls called lazily and scratched among the pebbles on the beach looking for tasty morsels left from picnics.

It was beginning to get dark, but a full moon and the lights along the harbour lit the scene.

Carl smiled at her. 'You are happy?'
'At this moment, yes.'
'Good.' He was satisfied. 'Here is The Albatross.'

*　　*　　*

The décor was a fresh blue, white and black. A huge model albatross was suspended over the bar, and the waiters — there were no waitresses — wore long white aprons as in old-fashioned French restaurants.

The food was superb, and Sorrel was glad to discover she still had a good appetite. She had been concerned that the scene with Marcus might have diminished it.

'No pasties,' Carl observed as they studied the menu.

'I should think not,' she said with mock indignation. 'They leave those for pasty shops and cafes. I think I'll have melon balls and raspberry sauce to start . . .'

'I also. In fact, I shall let you choose

the entire meal for me tonight,' he declared.

'But I might choose something you don't like!' she protested, amused.

'You will not. I shall like whatever you choose,' he returned placidly.

The balls of different melon fruit were accompanied by a sharp raspberry sauce.

'Mm — delicious,' they agreed as their empty plates were collected, every scrap having been eaten.

Next came little parcels of succulent chicken in filo pastry.

'I can see why this place has a good reputation,' she said approvingly, cutting into a parcel.

Carl poured more wine into her glass and nodded. 'I knew you would make a good choice,' he said.

For a few minutes they ate in silence, savouring the food, then Carl looked at her with a little frown.

'When I arrived at your shop, your friend Marcus was just leaving. I thought you looked a little upset. Was it something he had said?'

She stared at her plate. 'Can we finish this lovely food, then I'll tell you about it. I don't want to spoil the meal.'

He nodded. 'Of course.'

They chose nectarines in a maple syrup sauce to finish and then some fragrant coffee with little chocolates.

When they had finished Sorrel sat back with a deep sigh of complete satisfaction.

'That was the most wonderful meal. Thank you, Carl.'

He smiled with pleasure and reached for her hand, squeezing her fingers and raising them to his lips to give them a quick kiss.

'Thank you for coming with me. I have enjoyed it, too. Now, would you like to tell me what upset you?'

She had almost hoped he had forgotten. It was a pity to spoil the evening with her problems. But it would be good to talk it over . . .

She took the letter from her bag and passed it over.

He read it twice then handed it back.

'He is taking your shop from you? I have understood it correctly?'

She nodded. 'His sister, Pamela, is taking it. I discovered recently that she's the actual owner. She wants it for a wine bar.'

He drummed his fingers on the table and appeared lost in thought. Then he said, 'Have you appealed to her?'

She laughed bitterly. 'It would do no good. She's the sort of woman who always gets what she wants.'

'And I suppose in a small place like St Towan she doesn't have a great choice of suitable premises,' he reasoned.

'She says that my shop is the perfect site.'

Carl sat deep in thought as she drank her coffee. Then he asked, 'May I ask if you knew about this before we went to the Miniatura?'

She darted a quick glance at him. 'Please don't think I'm not serious about your suggestion for my shop.

Pamela *had* mentioned her wine bar, but she only wanted it because a friend of hers was opening one. I thought it would probably never happen. I hoped her enthusiasm wouldn't last.'

'Did Marcus speak to you about it?'

'Yes. But he was going to try to persuade her to find somewhere else. Since that hasn't worked, *I'm* the one who will have to start looking.'

'I see. So this is not a good time to ask you if you have made a decision about the miniatures?'

'It's not a good time for discussion about anything,' she said miserably. 'Tomorrow I'll go to the estate agent, but I don't have much hope of finding anywhere else.'

He took her hand again. 'Please don't make any quick decisions,' he said. 'I would hate you to disappear suddenly.'

She laughed. 'I shan't do that. And what about you? Shall you stay here in St Towan?'

'I, too, have not made a decision.'

'But you have a business in Bavaria.

202

Doesn't it need your attention?'

'Someone is looking after it for me,' he said vaguely. 'I can fly back if necessary. Now, shall we have another drink?'

Sorrel consulted her watch. 'I think I should be getting back. Work tomorrow.'

'You did enjoy our weekend?' he pressed.

She nodded. 'It was the break I needed. It took my mind off my problems. And I was very impressed with all you showed me.'

'I am pleased. Perhaps we could go somewhere again another weekend.'

'Perhaps,' she agreed as she stood up. 'But not yet.'

'Not yet,' he agreed and lifted a hand to summon the waiter.

It was dark when they left the restaurant. The moon had disappeared behind heavy clouds and the only light was the ring of street lamps around the harbour.

It was cold and the splash of waves

on the pebbles made it seem darker. There were few people about.

'I think it'll rain tomorrow.' She shivered, and Carl put his arm around her shoulders.

'If we walk so, you will be warm.'

She smiled at him. He was so thoughtful. Close together, they walked quickly in the direction of her shop.

★ ★ ★

Two evenings later, the telephone rang. When Sorrel answered it she found it was Carl.

'You have not found another shop?' he asked abruptly.

'No. There's nothing available.'

'I have had an idea,' he said. 'Shall I come to you or would you like to visit me for a change?'

'I'll come to you. I'll be with you in half an hour. Is it a good idea? Is it about the shop?'

'Wait till you get here and we shall discuss it.'

She was glad he lived near. The air was full of Cornish mizzle, the mixture of mist and drizzle which bedraggled the hair and gave clothes a damp and uncomfortable touch. She huddled into her waterproof jacket, turned up the hood and walked quickly up the hill.

Inside the cottage, Carl had built up a cheerful fire and pulled two armchairs near to its blaze. He took her coat and hung it at the side of the fire where it steamed gently.

On a table was a glass bowl filled with a rich red steaming liquid and some little glass mugs with handles.

'I found them in a cupboard,' he explained. 'For *glühwein*.' He handed her a glass. 'It will warm you up.'

'*Glühwein*?' She took an experimental sip, then another, and her face cleared. 'Ah, yes. We call it punch.'

'Punch?' He smacked a fist into his palm. 'That is a punch, *nein*? Not a very nice name for a warm, friendly drink!'

She laughed and settled herself in

one of the armchairs. He took the other, and for a few minutes they enjoyed the warmth of the drink and the fire. Then she looked at him inquiringly.

'So — you said you had a good idea?'

He took another drink and put the glass on the edge of the hearth where it would keep warm.

'You have had no success in finding a new shop,' he began. 'And as well as a shop, you need somewhere to live.'

She nodded. 'Yes. Ideally I'd like what I have now, a home behind and above the shop. Do you know of somewhere?' she asked, suddenly hopeful.

'Yes,' he said. 'Here.'

She looked around the little sitting-room of the cottage, then back at him. 'Here?'

He nodded. 'We should have to make a lot of alterations, of course, but it could be done. There is the workshop and the store-room and some outbuildings. We could make a cosy home and successful business premises.'

'But I don't have that sort of money,' she protested. 'Everything the shop earned went back into the business. It was the only way to build it up.'

'I have enough,' he said. 'Uncle Ernst left me some money. The business will belong to both of us, but I shall finance the alterations.'

'But that would make you a business partner,' she returned warily. 'I've never wanted a partnership. I like making the decisions. I like it to be my business.' She began to feel as if here was someone else trying to take her livelihood away from her. First Pamela and Marcus, now Carl.

'But it would be your business,' he soothed. 'I would just be there to help.'

'And another thing,' she rushed on. 'The cottage is very small. There is only the living-room and one bedroom. Where would I . . . ?'

Carl left his chair and in one fluid movement was kneeling beside her. He put his arms round her so that she couldn't move and pressed his lips to hers. For one short moment, she almost responded, then she pulled away. He mustn't propose to her, she didn't love him.

But a marriage proposal wasn't what he had in mind.

'My Sorrel,' he whispered. 'I love you. I think you could love me. And if we love each other, why do we need more than one bedroom?'

'But I don't love you,' she protested. 'And I don't want to marry you.'

'Marry!' he exclaimed and stood up. 'I did not mention marriage.'

She stood, too, and faced him, her eyes flashing. 'Then I'm sorry for misunderstanding you, but I could never live here with you if we were not married.'

'You are old-fashioned,' he smiled, trying to take her in his arms again. 'That sort of thing means nothing nowadays.'

'Maybe not to you but it does to me,' she said, moving away from him and putting on her coat. 'Thank you for trying to help me, but your idea wouldn't work. I'll solve the problem myself.'

As she turned towards the door, he barred her way. 'I hope this doesn't mean we can't work together,' he appealed.

'I'm still thinking about that. I'll be in touch. Goodnight, Carl.'

She marched back down the hill in a mood of fury and disappointment. Once again, Alyse's opinion of Carl seemed to be the right one.

A Bit Of A Shock

Alyse was very subdued for the next few days. The excitement over her trip to America seemed to have abated, and she sat quietly in the evenings working on her embroidery, not even listening to her story tapes. Sorrel was puzzled, and at last she questioned her about it.

'You're not afraid of the operation, are you?'

'Afraid? No, not at all.'

'Are you worried about the flight? I know you've never done a long trip before, but I don't think it'll be too bad.'

'No, I'm not worried about it at all.

'Oh, OK.' Sorrel turned again to the accounts she had spread across the dining-room table, but she couldn't concentrate.

'Alyse, I know something's wrong. Please tell me what it is.'

There was silence, then Alyse finally looked up, a glint of tears in her eyes.

'I can't go. I can't leave you with this awful problem about the shop. I must stay and help you.'

It had never occurred to Sorrel that her cousin could be worrying about her own problems.

'Of course you must go!' she exclaimed. 'I'll cope. I'll sort something out. And when you come back you'll be better and stronger. Then you can help me to move.'

'Are you sure?'

'Of course. I wouldn't dream of allowing you to turn down this opportunity. And Marcus would be so upset. He's determined that you'll get better.'

'Dear Marcus. He wants to help you too. He says he's certain he can find you another shop.'

Sorrel smiled. 'Carl wants to help too. When I went to see him the other evening, he came up with a suggestion.'

'Was it a good one?'

Her expression was pensive. 'He thinks I should move the business to his place. We'd adapt the workshop and outbuildings and I'd live in the cottage with him.'

That really caught Alyse's interest. 'Live in the cottage?' But it's tiny! You wouldn't have any room for yourself.'

'No.'

There was a moment's silence as Alyse figured it out.

'Oh, Sorrel, he asked you to marry him!' she exclaimed excitedly.

'No. He asked me to *live* with him.'

There was another silence, then Alyse said, 'He doesn't know you very well, does he?'

Sorrel grinned ruefully. 'Not very well at all.' She turned again to her accounts. 'I'll go to the estate agents in the morning to see if anything has come up. Then we'll ask Donna to look after the shop while we go shopping.'

Alyse sighed happily, unwound a skein of blue embroidery silk and cut a length. There was silence for half an hour as both girls concentrated on their activities and their own thoughts.

* * *

The visit to the estate agent was very short and very disappointing. 'Nothing, I'm afraid, Miss Basset,' he told her. 'We'll contact you the moment anything suitable comes up.'

She returned to the toyshop, collected Alyse and then they were on their way across the peninsula to Penzance. The busy town had lots of clothes shops and she was sure they would soon find all that Alyse needed.

They parked near the station and began slowly to climb Market Jew Street, studying the shop windows as they passed.

'Should I take nighties or pyjamas?' Alyse asked. 'Which do you think would be best for hospital?'

Sorrel considered. 'I don't know. Shall we buy two of each?'

With that they began to shop in earnest.

At the top of the street, they rested and reviewed their purchases. Nighties, pyjamas, dressing-gown, slippers — what else?

'A couple of comfortable leisure suits might be a good idea,' suggested Sorrel. 'They'll be easy to pull on and off. And some underwear.'

Alyse glanced up at the statue of a man looming above them. 'I hope he's not listening to us talking about underwear!' She giggled. 'He looks very serious. Who is he?'

'Humphrey Davy. He's holding a lamp, can you see? He invented the miner's safety lamp, the Davy lamp, in the nineteenth century. It must have saved countless lives underground. I believe they used naked candles before that.'

Alyse took another look at the statue, but her mind was really on their shopping project.

'Where now?' she asked.

'Coffee?' Sorrel suggested. 'There's a good place over there. Then we'll carry on.'

Alyse was glad to sink into a seat in the pleasant tea-shop.

'Is your hip painful today?' Sorrel asked anxiously.

'It doesn't like hills,' Alyse explained, then gave her a brave smile. 'But I keep telling myself that it won't be for much longer, thanks to Marcus.'

Two coffees and a couple of toasted tea-cakes later, they made their way down Chapel Street. A chemist shop provided a sponge bag and toiletries and another clothes shop had a good selection of underwear and leisure suits.

'I think that'll do, I don't think we can carry any more,' said Sorrel, 'and besides, you're beginning to look very tired. You've done a lot of walking. Come on, we'll head back to the carpark.'

★ ★ ★

Sorrel had hoped to go to the airport with Alyse to see her off, but two days before the departure, Donna's children went down with measles, so she was tied to the shop after all.

Alyse clung tearfully to her at the shop door as Marcus loaded her luggage into his car, then he settled her in the back seat with Mrs Goldman. Sorrel was pleased to see the wide smile with which Mrs Goldman greeted her. It was plain that her cousin would be well taken care of by this kindly American lady.

They were to stay at a hotel near Gatwick Airport overnight and fly out at ten the next morning. Marcus would stay with them and drive home as soon as they left.

Marcus was anxious to start the journey to London, so there was little time to talk, but before getting into the car, he came over to where Sorrel stood on the pavement, trying to catch a last glimpse of Alyse.

'May I call tomorrow and let you

know that Alyse has got away OK?' he asked.

'Of course. I hoped you would.' She knew she would be anxious to hear about Alyse; she just hoped he didn't take her enthusiastic answer personally.

Late in the afternoon, she had a visitor. Nicole Madron appeared in the shop, looking worried.

'No class this afternoon?' Sorrel asked. As well as conducting dance therapy classes at home, Nicole taught ballet to most of the children in St Towan at a studio in town.

'I've finished for today. I'm just on my way home from the studio. But I've heard something I think you should know.'

She sounded so concerned that Sorrel stopped what she was doing to look at her. 'What is it?'

'Sorrel, I have to ask you — how close are you to Carl Schumann?'

'Close?'

'You know — is there anything serious between you two?'

'What do you mean? We're friends, that's all.' She glanced at her watch. 'Look — it's nearly time to close. Go through and put the kettle on and we can talk in private. I'll be there as soon as I've closed up here.'

By the time she got through to the kitchen, Nicole was sitting at the table, a pot of tea in front of her and two mugs. She poured out and pushed one of the mugs across to her friend.

'Mrs Hinchman — she's the grand-mother of one of my little pupils — came to collect Annabel from her class this afternoon. She had spent the day in Truro and on the bus home she sat next to a young blonde girl.' Nicole paused, and the silence was heavy with something as yet unsaid.

'And?' asked Sorrel.

'They got into conversation,' Nicole went on. 'She was German.'

A cold feeling took hold of Sorrel. She didn't know what was coming next, and yet she felt a presentiment that perhaps she did.

'The girl told Mrs Hinchman that she was on her way to St Towan to visit her husband. It was to be a surprise. He was working in England and didn't know she was coming.' She paused. 'His name was Carl.' She looked at Sorrel. Sorrel gazed steadily back at her but said nothing.

Nicole's voice was quiet as she went on: 'She said they had been married for less than a year and she missed him.'

Sorrel was silent while she concentrated on her tea, then she said, 'What a good thing I didn't fall for him.'

'He didn't tell you he was married?' Nicole probed.

He very deliberately didn't tell me he was married, Sorrel thought, but she just said, 'No, he didn't mention it.'

Nicole regarded her anxiously. 'You've become very friendly. You went away with him.'

'That was business,' Sorrel retorted quickly. 'Strictly business. There's been nothing between us other than friendship.' She couldn't tell even Nicole about the mix-up over the hotel rooms or Carl's suggestion that she should move in with him at the cottage, especially not now.

'I expect his wife will be with him at the cottage now,' said Nicole. 'What are you going to do?'

'Oh, I'll wander up there later and make her acquaintance,' said Sorrel casually.

Nicole stood up. 'I'd better be on my way. Oh, I nearly forgot — what do you think of this?' She reached into her bag and brought out a brightly-painted wooden man about nine inches tall. He wore a shiny black bowler hat, a red coat and blue trousers, and had moving arms and legs.

Sorrel examined the toy with interest. 'It's good — though it's not one of Ernst's.'

'No. Carreg brought it home yesterday. It was made by the parent of one of his patients.'

Sorrel's eyes lit up. 'Really? How wonderful! It looks like Carreg might have found me a new toy maker! Thank him so much. If he gives me some details, I'll go and visit. Oh, Nicole, I'm so pleased!' Still smiling delightedly, she accompanied her friend to the door.

'How long will Alyse be away?' asked Nicole as she said goodbye.

'Probably six weeks. I'm missing her already.'

She went back into the kitchen and looked into the freezer. Alyse had left a selection of meals, carefully labelled. Taking one at random, she slid it into the microwave.

The next six weeks loomed ahead of her like a long, empty road. Alyse was a quiet girl, but still Sorrel valued her easy company, and now the house felt just too empty.

So, after dinner, she decided, she would do what she had told Nicole and go and visit Carl. It had to be done and sooner would be better than later.

★ ★ ★

She and Carl had an open-ended agreement to go for a drink on Wednesday evenings. If she wanted to go, she would stroll up to his house. If she didn't, she would stay at home.

She debated whether to dress up this evening, and then decided against it. After all, she wasn't in competition with his wife and she didn't want it to look as if she was.

She slipped on a pair of slate-blue, soft corduroy trousers and a white Angora jumper, fastened her hair into a plait at the back and applied the minimum of make-up, then she set off.

Halfway up the hill, however, she had second thoughts. Perhaps it would be better to wait until Carl brought his wife down to see her. But what if he didn't do that? What if he just sent her home?

She leaned on the wall and looked, unseeing, out across the waves. How could they continue to be friends with this between them? She would have to admit that she knew about his wife and there would be so much awkwardness. No, she had to go on and face him right now.

After just the faintest hesitation, she knocked briskly at the door of his cottage. Carl opened the door. In the background, she could see a girl, blonde and timid-looking, peeping out of the sitting-room.

He looked at Sorrel with an expressionless face, almost as if he didn't recognise her. He's had quite a shock, she thought.

'Good evening, Carl. It's Wednesday, remember?' she said smoothly.

'Oh, *ja*, Wednesday, of course.

'I wondered if you were going to take me — or your wife — out tonight?'

Carl passed a weary hand over his face, then held the door open and motioned her to enter.

'Please come in, we cannot talk here.'

The other girl stood near the fire in the sitting-room, nervously plucking at the edge of her jumper. Sorrel gave her a friendly smile.

'This is my wife, Ingeborg. Ingeborg, a friend of mine, Sorrel Basset.'

Sorrel held out her hand and after a moment's hesitation, the other girl clasped it. She was a pretty girl, as fair as Carl was dark. Her pale blue eyes were wary, and despite the fire her hand was cold. She looked upset. Obviously the reception from her husband hadn't been what she had expected.

'You knew my wife was here?' Carl asked Sorrel.

'Yes. As I've told you before, news travels fast in St Towan,' she said pointedly.

They all looked at each other, the silence fraught with undercurrents.

'I could make a drink,' Ingeborg suggested in a tentative tone. 'Coffee, perhaps?'

'Yes, do that,' said Carl.

When she had left the room, he motioned Sorrel to a chair and sat opposite.

'I don't know what to say,' he said. 'You must wonder why I've never mentioned Ingeborg.'

'On the contrary, Carl, I know exactly why you didn't mention that you're married.' She smiled and spoke pleasantly, but her words were direct. and she noticed that he couldn't meet her gaze. 'You were Ernst's nephew. I trusted you. But Ernst was fine and honourable and you are nothing like him.' Her lip curled with distaste as she spoke.

Ingeborg brought in a tray, and handed a cup of coffee to Sorrel, then one to Carl. She looked nervously at her husband but he ignored her. That annoyed Sorrel even more.

'Is this the first time you've been to England, Ingeborg?' Sorrel asked her.

'*Ja*. I have never been out of Germany before.'

Sorrel smiled kindly. 'You were very brave to come all this way alone then.'

The girl shrugged. 'I wanted to see Carl. We have been married less than a year. I missed him.'

Sorrel looked at Carl. Awkwardly, he reached out and took Ingeborg's hand.

'I've found a new toy maker,' said

Sorrel. 'I think it would be best if I continue with what I know. I'll not be changing from a toyshop — that is, if I can find somewhere for a new shop.'

She finished her drink and placed her cup on the tray, then stood up.

'Goodbye, Carl. It was — ' she hesitated ' — interesting, meeting you. Thank you for the trip to the exhibition. I hope you'll *both*,' she stressed, with a smile at Ingeborg, 'be very happy. She is a lovely girl,' she added to Carl.

He opened the door for her. 'Sorrel, shall we . . . '

'Goodbye, Carl. Goodbye, Ingeborg.' She walked quickly down the path and along the road without looking back.

She hoped she wouldn't meet anyone she knew. It would be hard to speak naturally when she felt so emotional — although it was difficult to know why she felt so sad. After all, Carl really meant nothing to her. Perhaps it was because a friendship had begun and ended in deceit. Thank goodness she hadn't really fallen for him.

When she got home, something made her open the door of Alyse's bedroom and gaze around. Everything was neat and in place. Alyse's perfume lingered faintly in the air.

Dear Alyse. She did so miss her, especially in the evenings when they usually sat together to chat about the day's events. If only she could have confided in her about this latest situation.

Closing the door, she went into the sitting-room, where she lifted Ernst's little swan from the mantelpiece and stroked the wooden feathers. Ernst gone, Alyse gone, Carl gone. She felt quite alone.

Then she gave herself a mental shake. Goodness, she was becoming maudlin! And Alyse would soon be back, healed and happy. She might even telephone home tomorrow.

★ ★ ★

The next evening, Sorrel went into the kitchen to put some clothes into the washing-machine. She would have to make a point of remembering to do this now; she was so used to Alyse taking charge of all the household chores.

As she came out of the kitchen, she stared at the telephone. Would Alyse ring her tonight?

As if in response to her hopeful question, the telephone began to ring and she snatched it up. Alyse?

'Sorrel — it's Marcus here.'

Of course, he had promised to report back on Alyse's departure.

'Oh, yes, Marcus. Thanks for phoning. Did they get away safely? With no delays?'

'Safely and dead on time at ten-oh-five this morning. They'll be in Dallas at half-past two — but, of course, that's American time. They're six hours behind us, so it'll be — what? — eight-thirty here?'

'I'm glad you worked that out for me!' she said gratefully.

'We had a comfortable hotel last

night,' he went on. 'Alyse was tired and a bit stiff from travelling, so she had an early night just after dinner.'

'Mrs Goldman seems very pleasant.'

'She's the best,' he agreed. 'She'll look after Alyse like a mother hen.'

They were talking like friends, Sorrel thought wistfully. She had so much to thank him for.

'Thank you again for looking after her . . . ' she began, but he cut her short.

'You've thanked me enough. If I see Alyse restored to perfect mobility, it'll all have been worth it.' There was a small sigh. 'I'm sorry, Sorrel, but I have to go. I must catch up on the work I've neglected for two days. I'll be in touch. Goodbye.'

She replaced the telephone and stood staring at it, thinking that he obviously didn't want to waste time chatting to her. Perhaps he was missing Alyse too.

Listlessly she went into the kitchen, made herself a cup of coffee and defiantly took two chocolate biscuits from the barrel.

A Perfect Evening...

Alyse rang early the next morning. 'Sorrel, are you managing without me? Did you find the meals in the freezer? They'll last you quite a while if you don't want to cook.'

'Thanks, Alyse, I'm managing fine. But never mind about me — how are you? You sound very near. I can't believe you're thousands of miles away.'

'Sorrel, this is the most beautiful house. I have a bedroom and a bathroom and a little sitting-room of my own. Imagine! Mrs Goldman is so kind. She treats me like a daughter.'

'When are you going to the hospital?'

'We're going to meet the doctors this afternoon and arrange for tests. I can't believe I'm really here in Dallas. I feel like a television star.'

She talked excitedly for a few more minutes then rang off, promising to telephone again when she had some news.

Happy that Alyse was happy, Sorrel began to prepare her breakfast. She had decided not to say anything to her cousin about Carl until it was necessary. Let the girl concentrate on her operation.

Before she could open the shop, the telephone rang again. This time it was Nicole.

'I wanted to catch you before you started work. Are you doing anything tomorrow night?' she asked.

'No, why? Would you like to come over?'

'Do you know the Lanyon Park Hotel?'

'I know it, but I've never been there. Someone has been spending a fortune on refurbishment, I believe.'

'Yes, but that's finished now and they're having a grand opening tomorrow. Carreg has been given some tickets. Would you like to come? It's a dinner dance. I thought you might like the chance to wear that lovely green dress.'

'But wouldn't you and Carreg prefer to go alone?' Sorrel protested half-heartedly.

'Not at all,' Nicole assured her. 'We want you to come. Please say yes.'

'All right. It's very kind of you, and I'd love it.'

'We'll pick you up by taxi at seven-thirty. See you!'

Sorrel replaced the receiver thoughtfully. She wouldn't have a partner; they would have to share Carreg. But perhaps there would be other people there she knew.

She glanced at the clock. Goodness, she'd have to hurry! Leaving the chaos in the kitchen for later, she dashed upstairs to finish her hair and make-up.

* * *

At lunchtime, she locked the shop door and went into town for some new eyeshadow and lipstick, but on her way up the main street, she collided with

232

Mrs Tregarron, who lived in the cottage next to Ernst's.

'Miss Basset, how are you? I haven't seen you for ages,' the lady exclaimed. 'Of course, I've noticed you visiting young Mr Schumann. Couldn't 'elp it really when I 'appened to be looking out of the window.'

Which was most of the time, thought Sorrel wryly.

The older woman grabbed her arm and held it in a tight grip. 'He's gone, did you know? Young Mr Schumann. Taken his wife and his belongings and gone. Went off early this morning. Place is all locked up. I shouldn't think he'll be coming back.'

'But why would he go off so suddenly?'

'I did 'ear,' Mrs Tregarron's voice lowered to a confidential murmur, 'that he'd been making up to quite a few young ladies in St Towan. Probably none of them knew about the wife. Put 'im in an awkward position, 'er turning up like that.'

If she'd hoped to disconcert Sorrel, she was unlucky.

'Well, thanks for telling me he's gone,' she said. 'I knew he wasn't staying long. Now, if you'll excuse me, I must finish my shopping. Goodbye.'

And she was off before Mrs Tregarron could say any more.

Sorrel carried on with her errands and chose her new cosmetics, but her thoughts weren't on make-up. So Carl had gone. Well, perhaps it was as well. They had no more to say to each other. She had enjoyed his friendship, but he had been dishonest with her and now she was glad he had gone.

But that meant his cottage was vacant! The thought struck her like a lightning bolt. It wasn't really what she wanted, but if there was nothing else, perhaps she could adapt it. She hurried down the street to the estate agent's.

'Nothing yet, Miss Basset,' he said before she could ask a question.

She smiled. 'Thanks, but I wanted to ask about the cottage on Fish Hill

— number six. I believe it's empty now.'

'Well,' he sounded reluctant. 'It *is* empty, certainly, but it's not up for sale. The owner wants to do it up before he puts it on the market. It wouldn't suit you in its present state.'

'Who is the owner? I'll contact him myself,' she suggested somewhat desperately. 'I dont want to lose it if it'll suit me at all.'

'Tell you what, Miss Basset I'll have a word with the owner, tell him you're interested and get him to phone you. How's that?'

It was obvious he didn't want to give her any details, so Sorrel had to be satisfied with that.

It occurred to her that perhaps the property was another one that belonged to Pamela Barrington. But the estate agent had said 'him' not 'her', when referring to the owner. And after all, even Pamela Barrington couldn't own all of St Towan!

★　★　★

Alyse telephoned again the next day. This time, she was more subdued. 'We went to see the surgeon,' she said, 'and I had all the tests.'

'Is there a problem? You don't seem so excited.'

'No. No problem. But I think I've realised at last that the operation is really going to happen. I'm not frightened, just apprehensive.'

'I'm sure you'll be fine,' Sorrel assured her. 'Did you like the surgeon? Is he young or old?'

'Young and gorgeous,' Alyse breathed. 'Just like a doctor in a film. Late thirties, I should think. Tall, fair and handsome. And so charming!'

'Well,' said Sorrel, 'such a paragon should help you to recover very quickly. When are you going in?'

'Next week. Mrs Goldman is going to take me out and show me something of the country while I'm waiting, so if you telephone and there's no reply, don't be surprised.'

'I'm glad you're having a good time

with Mrs Goldman. She sounds very kind.'

'She's an absolute gem,' Alyse agreed warmly. 'Are you doing anything exciting?' she asked, expecting her cousin to say no.

'Actually I'm going to a dinner dance tonight with Nicole and Carreg. It's a chance to wear my new green dress.'

'Where are you going?' Alyse queried, sounding interested.

'The Lanyon Park Hotel,' Sorrel told her, and sensed her surprised reaction.

'Oh, my goodness, you are moving in superior circles! Have they found you a suitably grand partner?'

'I shan't know till I get there, but I don't think so. I think I'm just to be with them.'

'Well, have a wonderful time. I'll be in touch.'

Sorrel enjoyed the preparations for her night out. It was the first time she had been somewhere really special for a long time. Of course, when she had been with Marcus . . . Determinedly she put that thought out of her mind. That was in the past.

She soaked for a long time in her best expensive bubble bath, then carefully made up her face to a level of glamour quite unknown in her everyday life. Satisfied, she brushed her hair until it swung loose and shining around her ears.

Jewellery was a problem. She had never possessed very much. She scanned her meagre collection with dismay. The dress needed very little adornment, but something beautiful would add the final touch . . .

Then she remembered. Reaching into a drawer of her dressing-table, she brought out a flat blue box. She gazed at it for a few moments before removing the lid.

Inside, on a bed of blue velvet, lay a silver and crystal bracelet. Within its circle were two delicate matching earrings. The set had been a present from Marcus on their first anniversary of going out together. When they had parted, she had put the jewellery in the box, placed it at the back of the drawer and never worn it again, nor even looked at it. She would have liked to return it to him, but she had wanted no contact, and certainly no argument, with him.

She lifted the bracelet from the box and held it against her dress. It was perfect. She fastened it around her wrist, then inserted the earrings. Finally she slipped her feet into the new pewter-coloured shoes and turned to regard her reflection in the wardrobe mirror.

A new Sorrel looked back at her, a graceful figure with shining hair and sparkling eyes. She gazed at her reflection wistfully. Wouldn't it have been wonderful if she had been going to the Lanyon Park Hotel with Marcus?

A knock at the front door broke into her reverie. Nicole and Carreg! She picked up a small beaded velvet bag which Alyse had discovered in a craft shop and presented to her, took one more quick glance at her reflection, and ran downstairs.

Outside, a taxi waited, its engine running.

'Mrs Madron said to take you to the Lanyon Park. She'll see you there,' the driver told her.

Carreg must have been held up at the hospital, she supposed.

She climbed in, and they were soon through the town and driving out along the coast road. Looking back, she saw the harbour below them, its lights stretched in a curve like a necklace, and she was reminded of the night she had looked at it from the car park with Carl. She wondered whether he would ever think of that night again.

The sight of the hotel, brilliantly illuminated in front of her, banished all thoughts of Carl from her mind. It was built in the Spanish style, with a tall tower in the centre rising from pantiled roofs. The windows were set into huge arches and the walls were painted gleaming white.

The taxi swept into the forecourt and she alighted in front of heavy iron-studded doors which stood open to receive the constant flow of guests.

At first she thought she would wait in the foyer for Nicole and Carreg. It was crowded with men in dinner jackets and women in colourful dresses, in pairs or groups, talking and laughing. She felt a little conspicuous on her own. She could see no one she recognised. But she saw with satisfaction that her dress was as lovely as any there.

She wandered over to where a fire burned brightly in a huge fireplace. On either side stood tall, wrought-iron candlesticks. Above the fireplace, a heavy ironwork mirror reflected the colourful scene. It was all very Spanish, she decided, though she had never visited that country.

Soon, people began to make their way to the dining-room. She looked around, her brow creasing slightly. There was still no sign of Nicole and Carreg. Perhaps she had missed them and they were already in the dining-room?

She approached the door where waiters were waiting to take guests' names and show them to their tables.

'Dr Madron's table,' she said a little diffidently.

The waiter motioned her to follow him, and they made their way between circular tables and blue upholstered chairs which matched the blue and gold carpet. He stopped on the far side at a table for two in front of an arched window.

A tall figure rose to his feet as she approached. Marcus!

The waiter held her chair and she sank into it in bewilderment.

'But where are Nicole and Carreg?' she asked.

'They're not coming. It's just us.' He looked levelly at her. 'Like old times.'

'But I don't understand. Nicole said . . . '

'Nicole said what I asked her to say. You wouldn't listen to me. I knew you would listen to her.'

'You mean — she tricked me?' Sorrel burst out.

'For the best of reasons,' he put in quickly. 'Would you have come if I'd asked you?'

There was a telling pause and he smiled wryly.

'No, I thought not.'

'Why didn't they come too?' she pleaded in a small voice. Perhaps the evening might have been easier to bear then.

'Carreg has a meeting tonight.'

Sorrel looked round the room. There were peals of laughter and a happy atmosphere. Waiters were beginning to serve the first course. What could she do — leave and cause a stir, or put a good face on it?

Marcus saw her dilemma. 'Can't you pretend? Can't we forget, just for one night?' Her hands were clasped in front of her on the tablecloth and he reached across and put a hand on hers. 'Please, Sorrel, let's try to enjoy ourselves

— like we used to.'

She looked up. His grey eyes regarded her beseechingly. He was so handsome. She loved him still, but he had hurt her so much. Could she forget? Might it happen again?

She was wearing a beautiful dress and had a handsome escort. For one night it might be possible to forget the past.

He moved his hand up her arm and stroked the bracelet with a fingertip.

She looked down. 'As you see, I still have it.'

'I'm glad.'

As the waiter slid a plate in front of her, she picked up her knife and fork and smiled at Marcus. 'I love Caesar salad,' she said, 'especially with avocado.'

Sensing her acceptance, Marcus visibly relaxed and picked up his wine glass. With a little nod of his head, he drank to her.

The main course was equally delicious. Roast duck was her favourite meat, and this time it was served with roasted vegetables and an unusual pepper and basil sauce. She enjoyed every mouthful and by the time they had finished, it had become as easy to chat away as if there had never been anything unpleasant between them.

By unspoken consent, neither mentioned the shop, or Pamela, or Carl. They talked of Nicole and Carreg and their lovely old house. They wondered how Alyse was enjoying America. Marcus told her how work was progressing at Pencarrock Barns and invited her to visit again.

By now, they had reached the plum frangipane tart with cream sauce. Sorrel sighed happily. 'I don't know when I've had such a wonderful meal.'

'Will you be able to dance?' Marcus teased. 'It would be a pity not to when you have such a perfect dress for it.'

She blushed and he smiled. 'Now don't blush,' he admonished. 'Red cheeks spoil the delicate green.'

She put her hands to her cheeks. 'Then don't tease me,' she scolded.

'I always loved to tease you . . . '

He realised what he had said and busied himself pouring more wine. Sorrel pretended she hadn't noticed the slip.

'Have you seen the swimming pool annex?' he asked. She shook her head. 'It's very pretty — palm trees and a mock beach with huge pebbles. I'll show you later.'

Coffee was served in the lounges which led off the central courtyard. The courtyard surrounded the tower and was filled with flowering shrubs. It was dark by now, so the whole scene was lit up by tiny lamps hidden amongst the bushes. Sorrel sat back in a squashy armchair and sighed.

'I feel so — comfortable.'

'Good,' he said. 'But don't get too settled. I want to dance.'

She knew she had been trying to postpone the moment when she would be held in his arms. She couldn't allow herself to realise how much she wanted that moment.

Eventually, though she tried to delay, her coffee cup was empty and Marcus drew her to her feet.

* ★ ★ ★

The next hour was bliss as they danced every dance. Marcus seemed unwilling to let her go and she felt that, in his arms, she was where she belonged.

At first they avoided looking into each other's eyes, but gradually reserve disappeared and his gaze held hers so that she couldn't look away.

At last he said, 'Would you like to see the pool? It might be cooler there.'

They peered through the glass walls into the pool area. The pool was oval in shape, the turquoise water reflecting the golden balls of the wall lights. It looked very romantic. Sorrel could imagine the sensation of swimming lazily up and down.

Marcus opened the door. 'Shall we go inside?'

A few chairs were occupied by

couples seeking privacy away from the crowds and Marcus and Sorrel walked to the far end and found two seats under a palm tree.

Sorrel giggled. 'I don't believe this! We're sitting under a palm tree by turquoise water. We should be in the South Seas.'

Marcus gazed at her. 'I'm happy right here. You look very beautiful.'

'Accept compliments gracefully,' she remembered her mother always saying, but it was no use, she felt embarrassed.

'It's the dress,' she said. 'It's very glamorous.'

'The person inside the dress makes it glamorous,' he corrected softly.

She was silent. He took her hand. 'Have you nothing to say?'

'Yes. I think we should have some coffee to sober us up.'

She tried to look away from him, but his gaze held hers like a magnet.

'I'm quite sober. I know exactly what I'm saying. I'm telling you I'm still in love with you.'

'And your wife?' she whispered.

'She's not my wife now. She only was for a very short time, years ago. It was a mistake. Oh, Sorrel, you know all this.'

She stood up. 'It's been a wonderful evening. Thank you so much. But perhaps we should go home now. I have work to do tomorrow and I'm sure you have too.'

He stood too and put his arms lightly around her. 'I don't want this evening to end. Could we . . . could we do it again?'

She moved away from him. 'I don't know. I don't know what I want. It'll take time. Memories . . .'

Agitated, she began to walk towards the door, but he caught up with her and pulled her into his arms again.

'Sorrel, stay a little longer, please. We could dance again.'

'No I must go now, Marcus.' Her voice was determined. 'If you're staying, could you get me a taxi?'

'We'll both go. I don't want to stay here without you.' He was disappointed but resigned. 'I didn't bring my car. I'll go and arrange a taxi.'

In the taxi, they sat in silence. She had no desire for the evening to end in disappointment. She had had such a lovely time.

She turned towards him, at the same moment as he reached for her. His lips found hers and his kiss was fierce and searching.

'Oh Sorrel,' he murmured against her hair, 'my Sorrel. Please say we've found each other again.'

The taxi slowed to a stop. She sat up and hurriedly searched for her bag which had fallen from her lap.

'Let me come in,' he begged. 'I won't stay long.'

'No. I don't think that would be wise. We'll be in touch.' She thanked him again and was out of the car and slamming the door almost before he realised she had gone.

Inside the house, she leaned against the door and closed her eyes. What now?

★ ★ ★

Nicole called in next day on her way home from ballet class. She popped her head round the shop door with an expression of mock apprehension.

'I don't know how you dare come here,' Sorrel scolded her, 'tricking me like that.'

'But you enjoyed the evening,' said Nicole. 'I've heard all about it from Marcus.'

Not all, I hope, thought Sorrel. Not that I let down my defences and returned his kiss so passionately . . .

'He said you had a lovely evening,' Nicole went on. 'Beautiful food, dancing cheek to cheek, sitting out by the pool . . . All so romantic. I knew it would work out.'

'Hold on,' said Sorrel. 'It was a lovely evening, yes, but we were both making the best of a difficult situation.'

'Difficult situation?' Nicole hooted. 'That's not how he described it! When are you going out again?'

251

'We're not. At least, we haven't arranged anything.'

Nicole's expression showed her disappointment. 'And I thought I'd kickstarted your romance.'

'Thank you for your efforts but please let me manage my own romance,' Sorrel pleaded. 'Would you like a coffee?'

'Can't stay, I'm afraid. I have a private class at four-thirty. Oh, Carreg sent you this.' She took a piece of paper from her pocket. 'It's the name and phone number of that toy maker. 'Bye.'

Sorrel watched from the window as her friend darted gracefully down the street and disappeared round the corner towards the harbour and her dance studio.

Dear Nicole. She had interfered for the best of reasons. But please don't let her set up any more meetings with Marcus just yet, Sorrel prayed. The scene in the taxi was too fresh in her mind for her to face him calmly.

He phoned the following day. She was busy and her answering machine took the message. It was brief: he said he had enjoyed their evening very much and reminded her that he hoped she would go out with him again. Would she please ring him?

She decided to wait for a few days before returning the call. Where Marcus was concerned, her mind was still in turmoil.

Misunderstandings...

A few days later, Sorrel received a telephone call from Mrs Goldman in Dallas. She was sure Sorrel would be delighted to hear that 'dear Alyse' had had her operation and that as far as it could be ascertained at this early stage, it had been successful.

'Of course, this is something of an experimental operation,' she said. 'Only Mr Jackson is performing it at present and he hasn't done more than a dozen.'

'But Alyse knew that, didn't she?' said Sorrel. 'She was prepared to take the risk.'

'She certainly was,' said Mrs Goldman. 'She's a brave little girl. Now we must all keep our fingers crossed.'

'Thank you for all you're doing for her, Mrs Goldman,' said Sorrel. 'I don't know how she would manage without you.'

'I have no children of my own, although I wanted them,' Mrs Goldman confided. 'I have known Alyse for only a few weeks, but she's like a daughter to me. I'll be so unhappy when she goes back to England. And between you and me, I think someone else will miss her, too,' she added in a teasing tone.

'Someone clse? But she doesn't know anyone else in America,' Sorrel protested.

'She didn't — but she does now,' Mrs Goldman returned with a happy laugh. 'Her surgeon, Mr Jackson, is *most* taken with her. He visits several times a day and stays chatting as long as he can.'

Sorrel wasn't sure what to make of this. If the operation had been experimental, the man responsible would be bound to take a close interest in its outcome. But Mrs Goldman seemed to think he had a more personal interest.

'Well, as long as he makes her better, I don't care how often he visits,' Sorrel said. Then a thought occurred to her.

'Does Marcus know it's been a success?'

'I've already telephoned Marcus, and Mr Jackson will be sending him a report. And Alyse told me to tell you that she'll be sending you a long letter as soon as she can.'

'Tell her not to worry. I know she's in good hands. I just want her to rest and get better.'

Sorrel replaced the receiver and sat thinking of Alyse in her hospital bed. If only she could be with her. But Mrs Goldman was filling her place very well, she was sure.

She picked up the phone again and dialled Donna's number. She would want to know that Alyse had come through the operation safely.

★ ★ ★

Sorrel had been waiting in vain for the estate agent to let her know about Carl's cottage and decided to go and see him. He looked up guiltily when she entered his office.

'Ah, Miss Basset, I was going to phone you.'

'Yes, I've been waiting,' she said, not believing him.

'I had a word with the owner. As I told you, he has some plans for the premises.'

'But did you make it plain that I'm interested?'

'I did, but he doesn't want to sell yet.' He looked unhappy, as if he didn't like being evasive about the sale. And suddenly Sorrel realised why. He was afraid she would guess the name of the owner. And she *had* guessed.

'It's Marcus Barrington, isn't it?' she demanded.

His expression showed she had guessed right. 'Please, Miss Basset, he doesn't want to discuss this property.'

But Sorrel was out of the shop before he had finished speaking.

She marched home in a fury. Marcus knew she desperately needed a shop. He had kept quiet about the fact that he owned Carl's place and that it was now available. Was Pamela behind this too? Had she had another bright idea for a business? And just a few evenings ago, he'd said that he loved her!

Still in a fury, she dialled his number. He answered straight away.

'Sorrel, how lovely to hear you. You got my message?'

'Never mind that. I want to speak to you about the cottage on Fish Hill — Ernst Schumann's cottage. Does Pamela own that too?'

'No, it's mine. I bought it from her.'

She was taken aback for a moment.

'You — bought it from her? Why?'

'Because I had an idea about it. But I didn't want to say anything until I found out if it was feasible.'

She was so angry she barely heard his words.

'You knew I wanted another shop,' she stormed. 'You said you would help me. Why didn't you say that the place belonged to you? You could at least have given me a chance to decide if it was suitable or not. How could you say you love me? I think you want to drive me out of St Towan!'

As she slammed down the telephone, frustration, disappointment and loneliness welled up inside, and she burst into tears.

There was a loud knock at the door. Hastily she dried her eyes. Who could that be? She must look a mess. She glanced in the hall mirror. Yes, her eyes were red and her cheeks blotchy.

There was another knock. With a deep sigh, she went to the door and opened it. Tony Redvers stood there.

He took one look at her face and folded her in his arms. 'What is it? Not — not Alyse?'

'No, it's all right,' she sniffed, 'Alyse is fine. It's nothing. I just felt low.'

'And I haven't helped, have I? I've been neglecting you. But I can make amends now. What are you doing today?'

'Well,' she moved out of his arms and gestured around vaguely. 'Housework, I suppose. And I have a few things to do in the shop.'

'It's half-day, isn't it? OK — get yourself ready, I'm taking you out.'

'Taking me out? But where?'

'St Michael's Mount. It'll blow your cobwebs away. When did you last go there?'

'Oh, ages ago. Tony, that would be so nice! Give me ten minutes,' and she fled upstairs, her spirits rising again.

'Warm trousers and flat shoes,' he called up to her. 'Remember the cobbled paths and steep climbs.'

She splashed cold water on her face to banish the traces of her recent tears, brushed her hair, tied it back, and was ready.

'The car's at the station car park,' he said when she rejoined him. 'Come on, we must catch the tide while it's still out then we can walk across the causeway.'

★   ★   ★

The little town of Marazion was on the opposite coast to St Towan. In half an hour, they were sweeping into its carpark. The town faced the island which was St Michael's Mount. In the soft sunlight of an autumn day, the castle could be seen clearly, its towers and chimneys rising above the wooded hill on which it was built.

They set off down the Marazion beach and on to the cobbled causeway which led to the island.

'Be careful, the rocks are uneven and you don't want to slip,' Tony warned, taking her arm.

They were buffeted by the sea winds but it was exhilarating walking across a causeway which would, in a few hours, be deep under the waves. At last they climbed the slope at the side of the harbour wall and were on the island.

Sorrel looked back at the mainland. 'How long is the causeway?'

'About four hundred yards. Not far.' He took her hand. 'Come on, let's have a coffee to warm us up before we look around.'

Across the café table, Sorrel smiled at him. 'I'm so glad you thought of this. It's just what I needed.'

'Do you want to tell me why you were upset?' he asked diffidently. He was concerned, but he didn't want to pry.

'You know half the story — that Pamela intends to take my shop — so you might as well know the rest.' She sighed. 'There's nothing suitable in St Towan for another shop. Then Carl Schumann left old Ernst's place abruptly and I tried to get that. It's not quite what I wanted but I'm desperate. The estate agent told me that the owner has plans for it. And the owner turns out to be — '

'Marcus Barrington,' he finished for her. 'I know, Pamela told me.'

'Did she tell you why he wants it?'

'No, but I have an idea.'

She waited, looking inquiringly at him.

'Well, it's pretty obvious, isn't it?' he said.

'Not to me. Tell me.'

He looked away. 'I'd rather not say. I could be wrong, but . . . Don't be too hard on Marcus.'

'I already have been.' She smiled ruefully. 'I shouted at him and slammed down the phone.'

'Oh, dear.' He made a face. 'Well, we'll just wait and see.' He stood up. 'Come on, let's go up to the castle.'

The café, houses and shops faced the tiny sheltered harbour. Behind them, a cobbled path known as the Pilgrim's Steps climbed sharply between rocky gardens full of seaside plants and windblown palm trees.

'I love this place,' said Tony as they rested and looked back at the sea below. 'Last year, I visited Mont St Michel, off the Brittany coast. It's similar but a much larger version of this. But I prefer this one. The French island is commercialised and brash, whereas this still has the feeling of the monastery it once was.'

For the next hour, they toured the rooms, studying the weaponry and furniture and paintings.

'It was a fortress in the time of Henry the eighth and in the Civil War,' Sorrel related from the notices around the walls. 'Now it's a castle and a private home. What a romantic place to live.'

'Rather wild in the winter, mind,' said Tony. 'When the tide surrounds the island, you're completely cut off.'

'Mm. In your own little world,' she said dreamily. 'Sounds appealing.'

Outside the castle again, she shivered. 'It's getting cold. We're very high up, aren't we?'

He took her hand. 'Come on, it's all downhill now. Let's go and get another warm drink before we tackle the causeway again.'

Once more in the café, hands wrapped round a comfortingly hot cup, Sorrel asked the question that had occurred to her several times since Pamela's fall from Marcus's horse outside the shop.

'What about you and Pamela?'

He met her gaze steadily. 'What about us?'

'Would she mind if she knew we were here together?' she pressed.

'You and I are old friends. Why should she mind?'

She looked at him without speaking, and he shrugged. 'There's nothing between Pamela and me — now.'

'But there was?'

'For a while,' he conceded. 'She's an attractive girl, but if I'm honest, not really my type. And she offered me a job when I was looking for one.'

'To manage her wine bar?'

'Yes. I was pleased at first, but then it didn't seem right — taking your shop. I felt uncomfortable about it.'

'Why didn't you come and talk to me?'

'Several reasons. I felt embarrassed. And you had become friendly with Carl Schumann. And there was always Marcus. I didn't know if I'd be welcome.'

'You're my oldest friend in St Towan. You'll always be welcome,' she said with feeling. 'But what are you going to do about another job?'

'I've got one,' he said triumphantly. 'I'm going to manage a hotel in Falmouth.'

'Oh, Tony, I'm so pleased for you. You must take me to see it sometime.'

'I will. Now, tell me how Alyse has got on in America,' he said.

They chatted about Alyse till Tony suddenly looked at his watch. 'Quick! The tide will be in. They'll close the causeway.'

He grabbed her hand and they raced along the harbour road to where the causeway began. But they were too late. A chain hung across the entrance and they could see the tide coming in fast.

'Too late,' he said. 'It'll have to be the ferry boat.'

They walked along the harbour wall to where two small boats were bobbing perilously as people scrambled aboard. They found places in the second boat

266

and were soon pulling away from the island.

'It's been a lovely afternoon, Tony,' she said.

'I've enjoyed it too,' he replied. 'When we land, shall we find something to eat?'

'I've got a better idea. Come back with me and I'll make us supper. Do you like omelettes? My cooking isn't in the same league as Alyse's, but even I can manage an omelette!'

Later, after supper, when Tony had gone, Sorrel sat deep in thought. She had realised her childhood dream, created her toyshop, enjoyed herself for several years — was it time to do something else?

Alyse would come back well, and able to make a new life for herself. Perhaps she would move away. Or perhaps the two cousins could start a different business together somewhere else. Unless Marcus had plans for Alyse.

There was an alternative, of course.

Sorrel could move to Australia and be with her family again. She missed them, and her mother often suggested that she should sell up and join them on the other side of the world.

But as she'd told Alyse, she couldn't imagine living anywhere but Cornwall. She loved it so.

She moved across to look out of the window. It was too dark to see, but she could hear the slap of waves on the rocks. This was her special part of the world. She would never leave it.

The best idea might be to look for a business in a nearby town. It would be a wrench to leave St Towan, but she needn't move far away.

She turned the problem round and round in her mind until, tired of thinking about it, she found a simple, uncomplicated book, and took it to bed.

★　★　★

Marcus made no attempt to contact her for several days. Was he sulking?

Not very likely; he wasn't that sort of man. Was he upset and offended by her attack on the telephone? Possibly, and she realised that he had every right to be. She should at least have given him a chance to explain.

Or had he decided she wasn't worth helping? That was her fault too. Why should she assume she had an automatic right to any empty property in St Towan?

On reflection, she knew she should apologise. She had been in the wrong. So she wrote a short letter acknowledging that her response had been excessive and that he had a perfect right to do as he liked with his own property. Then, during a quiet moment in the shop, she dashed out and posted it before she could change her mind.

Two days later, she looked up from wrapping a customer's parcel to find Marcus in the shop. As calmly as she could, she completed the transaction and bid the customer goodbye. Then she turned to Marcus.

'I got your letter,' he said.

She looked at him, her fingers playing nervously with a pencil on the counter.

'Surely you know me well enough to realise that if I said I would help you, then I meant it,' he went on. 'To accuse me of trying to drive you from St Towan was unkind and ridiculous.'

'I've said I'm sorry.' She wasn't going to grovel.

'I've had people at the cottage on Fish Hill deciding whether it would be possible to convert it in a suitable way for your business,' he told her.

So that was what Tony had meant. He had guessed how Marcus wanted to help her. Yet she, who thought she loved him, had so little faith.

'I'm sorry,' she said quietly, 'I should have guessed. You're very generous.'

'I'll let you know if I get a positive report about it.' There was no warmth in his voice. He was obviously still upset.

'Thank you,' she said as they moved towards the door.

On the threshold, he stopped. 'I've

had a telephone call from Mrs Goldman and a report from the surgeon in Dallas. They say Alyse is doing very well, which is wonderful news. I'll be in touch, Sorrel. Goodbye.'

She stared at the door long after he had gone. What would he be thinking of her now? He wouldn't go back on his promise to help her, but he wouldn't do it with much enthusiasm. She was driving him into Alyse's arms. Her cousin would return from America, grateful and loving towards Marcus, and he would be lost to her for ever.

If a customer hadn't entered the shop at that moment, she would have burst into tears.

★　★　★

The little painted man in the bowler hat which Carreg had got for her, had been watching her from a shelf in the kitchen ever since Nicole had brought him to her. Now she took him down and studied him.

He was bright and well painted, and his arms and legs moved smoothly. Whoever had made him would be a worthy successor to Ernst. She was determined to go and find him.

Donna's children had recovered from their attack of measles and she was happy to look after the shop once more. So one fine autumn morning, Sorrel drove out of St Towan, along high-banked lanes, into the heart of the Cornish countryside. Deserted lanes criss-crossed each other in bewildering fashion and she had difficulty in following the directions Carreg had given her over the telephone. However, at last she saw a sign pointing to Polskiddy and turned in that direction.

Polskiddy was a tiny hamlet with a church, a post office and a few houses. Obviously there would be more houses in the lanes around the village, but Carreg had suggested that she ask for final directions at the post office.

'Walnut Cottage? Yes, it's Mr Kehellan

you'll be wanting then. Come and I'll show you.'

The obliging woman who served in the shop part of the post office took her outside and gestured to a hill. 'Down there. 'Tis very steep. Turn right at the bottom. Follow the stream and you'll come to the cottage.'

Sorrel thanked her, returned to her car and began to drive carefully down the hill, which certainly was very steep. Walnut Cottage was a hundred yards from the bottom of the hill.

She parked in the yard in front of the cottage and climbed out. The atmosphere was still and timeless. The little cottage with its uneven roof tiles and tiny windows must have stood here for hundreds of years. Sorrel stood still, drinking in the tranquillity of the scene.

But then, suddenly, a raucous snatch of singing broke the stillness: 'Singing willow, tit willow, tit willow . . . ' It came from a small building next to the cottage.

The door was propped open and

cautiously she approached and peeped in. A young man with the brightest mop of red hair she had ever seen was sitting at a workbench, deftly carving a piece of wood. He sang happily in his dreadful voice as he worked.

Suddenly aware that he was being watched, he looked up and the song ceased mid-line as he and Sorrel stared at each other.

She held out the wooden man. 'Dr Madron said . . . ' she began.

He stood up and rubbed his hands on his jeans.

'Ah, you're the young lady Dr Madron mentioned to me. You've got a toyshop in St Towan.'

'Yes. I wondered whether I could see some more of your work.'

'Of course. Sorry about the singing. My wife stops me when she's here, but she's out shopping so I let rip. My grandad played Gilbert and Sullivan records non-stop when I was a nipper so I learned all the words.' He smiled sheepishly. 'I love singing.'

Sorrel laughed. 'It's nice to hear someone so happy.'

'Come through here.' He led the way into another small room behind his workshop. On shelves around the walls were ranged wooden toys of every description. It was almost like being back with Ernst again.

'How wonderful!' She turned to him. 'Did you happen to know Ernst Schumann?'

'I'll say!' he said. 'I lived next door to him when I was young. It was Ernst who started me on this.'

Sorrel felt tears behind her eyes. It was as if Ernst had guided her towards her new toy maker.

'Ernst made toys for my shop,' she explained. 'Now he's gone, I'm looking for someone else.'

'If you like my work, I'd be happy to oblige. Look around, there's no rush.' He looked at his watch. 'I usually stop for a coffee about now. Would you like one?'

'Lovely — thanks.'

When he'd gone Sorrel began to examine his work in earnest. His characters were slightly more modern than the old German toy maker's, but still simple and finished in bright, primary colours. The collection included games and puzzles and travelling toys. She especially liked a sparkling yellow pull-along duck with a nodding head.

She was playing with this when he returned with two mugs of coffee.

'That's a new one,' he said. 'Only finished it yesterday.'

He found two stools, and brushing sawdust off the top of one, placed it for Sorrel. Perching on the other, he gave her his infectious grin. 'Well? What have you decided?'

'I love your stuff. It's exactly what I'm looking for. So I'd like to buy several things today and give you an order for next month,' she said. 'Would that be satisfactory?'

'I can't make exclusively for you,' he warned, 'but I don't have another customer anywhere near St Towan.'

Sorrel finished her coffee and they went into the cottage to complete the financial side of the arrangements.

Later, as she drove back to the shop, she felt happier than she had done for some time and full of positive energy. She would not go to Australia; she would find another shop and make it even better than the one she had at present.

She was greeted with, 'There's a letter from America,' when she entered the shop. It was plainly from Alyse and Donna was excited and eager to know what she had to say.

Sorrel tore it open and began to read aloud: ' 'There's so much to tell you, I don't know where to begin. I've left hospital and I'm recuperating at Mrs Goldman's house. When I'm well enough to walk, we're going to her summer place, *by the ocean*, as she calls it. She really is a lovely person'.'

There were two more pages about Mrs Goldman and what they were doing and what they were going to do.

Then: ' 'Mr Jackson — Robert — calls in almost every day. We get on so well. Mrs Goldman is thinking of taking a few friends with us to her holiday home and she's going to ask Robert if he can get away'.'

Sorrel and Donna looked at each other with raised eyebrows, then Sorrel read on: ' 'Sorrel, it's so wonderful! I came to America for an operation and I believe I've found love. You'll say I'm silly, that it's what women often feel when they have an attractive surgeon, but it's not like that. We haven't said anything to each other, but I can feel it. I love him and I'm sure he loves me'.'

Sorrel looked at Donna over the top of the letter. 'You can't fall in love as fast as that — can you?'

'It probably is just infatuation,' said Donna. 'She'll forget all about him when she gets back here.'

And when she gets back, Marcus will be waiting for her, Sorrel thought. What will they do? How will it all work out? What a tangle! I love Marcus, Marcus loves Alyse, and Alyse thinks she loves her surgeon.

She folded the letter and returned it to the envelope, Donna watching her thoughtfully.

'Don't worry about it,' she said comfortingly. 'It'll work out. Tell me how you got on this morning. Did you find your new toy maker?'

★   ★   ★

The next day brought a letter with a German postmark. There was no need to look at the signature to discover the sender.

'*My dear Sorrel,*' Carl wrote. '*I could not disappear from your life without saying how sorry I am for our hurried departure. At the time, I felt I could not face you again. My behaviour in England was not good. I can only say that when I met you, I quickly became very fond of you and I felt that you were beginning to have some warm feelings for me. As time went on, it* became harder to say what I knew I should say.

'When Ingeborg arrived, I could not think how to explain to you so it seemed best to leave your so pleasant little town.

'Please do not think I do not love my wife. Inge is a sweet girl. I love her and we shall be happy together. She asks nothing about my time in England. She liked you and was pleased I had a friend.

'My address is not on this letter so you will not be worried to reply.

'My best wishes for your future, my thanks for the past. Carl Schumann.'

The Letter

Sorrel had an urgent desire to see what was happening at Ernst's old cottage. Perhaps if she went round there, she could find someone to ask.

At lunchtime, she locked the shop door and made her way up Fish Hill, but as she leaned against the sea wall and stared at the cottage across the road, there was no sign of any activity.

She thought of the number of times she had entered that front door. She had visited Ernst there, then Carl. Would her next visit be as prospective owner?

She studied it speculatively. Small cottage, small outbuilding. Could it ever be made into a bright welcoming toyshop? She doubted it.

As she mused, a figure came out of the front door and locked it behind him. He walked down the path, deep in thought, then looked up and saw her.

'Sorrel. What are you doing here?'

'Hello, Marcus. Just looking — and thinking.'

'Have you had lunch?'

'No.'

'Come and have something with me.'

'Thanks, but I can't. I have to open again at two.'

'Not even a pasty at the Schooner? We could walk there in a few minutes.'

Thinking of Carl's letter and her visit to the Schooner with him, she shook her head. 'Not even that.'

'Sorrel, do you remember the night at the Lanyon Park when I asked you if we could do it again — go out for a meal? What do you think? A night out would cheer us both up.'

Of course, he was miserable without Alyse, she thought. But she said, 'Cheer us up?'

'I'm afraid the news about the cottage isn't good. My idea won't work. The building can't be altered in such a way that it would give you the sort of place you want.'

'It's funny,' she said, 'I was just thinking that myself.'

He drew her arm through his and they walked slowly down the hill.

'Don't be too upset. I'm still looking for somewhere. We have plenty of time. Pamela has gone to London to work with her friend and get some experience of wine bars, so she won't want your place for several months.'

Sorrel felt herself relax. Somehow she'd had the feeling that her departure from The Toybox was imminent.

As they reached the bottom of the hill, he turned to face her. 'Tonight? Dinner?' he pressed.

'All right. Thank you.'

'Have you any preference as to where we go?'

She considered. 'I'd like to visit La Cenerentola again. Alyse and I went there on her birthday.'

For a moment she thought there might be a response to her cousin's name, but he just said, 'Good. I like it there, too.'

Marcus picked her up at seven giving her plenty of time to prepare. She decided to wear a long black skirt and one of the new tops she had bought on her shopping expedition to Truro, one made of white cotton lace with long tight sleeves. She felt she looked elegant and quite smart enough for the chic La Cenerentola.

Marcus smiled his approval. 'I like your hair piled up like that. It makes you look quite different.'

'Different from what?'

'Oh, your everyday look, I suppose. You're usually much more casual.'

'If I haven't stuck in enough pins, it'll fall down and I'll have that casual look again,' she said, and they both laughed. It was a good to start an evening, she thought, compliments and laughter.

Marcus had reserved a table close to the dance floor. Sorrel had forgotten there was a dance floor when she had suggested La Cenerentola. Now she began to regret her choice. Dancing with Marcus would bring back too many memories. And she had enjoyed it too much at the Lanyon Park Hotel.

But that had been an evening on its own. Making the best of a difficult situation, as she'd told Nicole . . .

She realised Marcus was speaking to her.

'Oh, sorry — what was that?'

He smiled. 'You were miles away. I asked what you'd like to drink.'

They gave their orders and were handed menus. Sorrel studied hers, then, glancing over the top of it, found Marcus smiling at her.

'I can't believe we're really here,' he said. 'It's quite like . . . '

'Please, don't say it's like old times,' she said quickly. 'We can't recreate the past. This is different, this is now.'

'I stand rebuked,' he said, but a smile played about the corners of his mouth.

'This place really is spectacular for Cornwall,' he commented, appraising the statues and the splashing fountain.

'It's not quite what one expects in the Celtic west.' He looked down at his menu. 'Have you chosen?'

'Not yet, though I know what I don't want — I don't really want pasta, or soup.'

'What about risotto? It's delicious here, with wild mushrooms.'

'Mm. That sounds nice — all right.'

'And for the main course?'

'I had lamb last time so I want to try something different. Any suggestions?'

'Their speciality is a chicken dish cooked with white wine and cream and herbs. I've tried it and it's delicious.'

'Then I'll try that,' Sorrel agreed. 'And I'll leave the wine to you. You know much more about that than I do.'

The wine waiter was called and had a long discussion with Marcus. Sorrel was more than satisfied with the result; the wine she was served was perfect.

'Italy is best-known for some famous red wines,' said Marcus, 'but this is a very acceptable white. You prefer white, don't you?'

He seemed to remember so much . . .

Sorrel sipped her wine and looked around the restaurant. There wasn't a face she knew anywhere. She turned back to Marcus. What were they going to talk about tonight? Not the shop, that was a sore subject.

'I wonder how Alyse is progressing?' he said.

Of course, Alyse.

'She's made a very good start,' he went on. 'She should be home in a few more weeks — if Mrs Goldman will let her go.' They both laughed.

'She's the daughter Mrs Goldman never had,' Sorrel remarked, 'and thoroughly enjoying every minute of it, I'm sure.'

'And what about the surgeon?'

'The surgeon?' she echoed. What did he know about him?

'Mrs Goldman writes that he's very taken with Alyse,' he expanded. 'I hope he doesn't upset her.'

'Why should he do that?'

'Well, if it's no more than a kind of

holiday romance, I suppose.'

Sorrel studied his face. Was he really worried that Alyse would find someone else to love? If only she really knew what he felt about her cousin.

Suddenly Marcus jumped to his feet. 'Look who have just come in.' He waved to a couple standing near the door and looking round as if for a table. 'It's Nicole and Carreg.'

Sorrel felt a great surge of relief as the other couple approached. Now she could enjoy the evening without worrying about making conversation with Marcus.

Waiters bustled around laying two more places and their friends were soon settled at their table.

'This is a surprise,' said Nicole, looking from Sorrel to Marcus with sparkling eyes.

'And we didn't need your trickery, either,' said Marcus with some amusement. 'Sorrel agreed to come out with me of her own free will.'

Sorrel blushed. 'Well, I had to eat

somewhere. What are you two doing here?'

'Carreg finished early for once so we grabbed the opportunity for an evening out.'

★ ★ ★

Later, looking back on the evening, Sorrel couldn't remember when she had enjoyed herself more. They ate and drank and laughed and danced. Even dancing with Marcus wasn't the ordeal she had feared. The presence of their friends had lightened the intensity of the evening.

★ ★ ★

For a week life was uneventful. Sorrel opened the shop in the morning and closed it at night. Customers came and went. She spent the evenings doing housework or watching television, waiting for Alyse's return.

There had been one short telephone

call from her cousin saying that she was feeling stronger and walking better every day.

Then came the bombshell. A bulky letter with an American stamp came through the letterbox and fell with a thump on the carpet. Sorrel picked it up and examined it with a sense of foreboding.

She waited with impatience until the evening so that she would have time to read it without fear of interruption. She took a cup of tea upstairs to her sitting-room, settled herself in an armchair and began to read.

The first few lines gave her such a shock that she had to go back and read them again slowly.

'Dearest Sorrel,' she read. 'This will be such a shock, I know, so I'll come straight out with it. I'm married! I'm now Mrs Robert Jackson. Yes, my lovely surgeon. So fairy tales do come true.

'I couldn't believe at first that he could feel about me the way I felt about *him, but when he asked me to marry him, I knew he loved me, too.*

'Please be happy for me. Mrs Goldman is thrilled, though she thinks perhaps we should have returned to England for the wedding. But we just couldn't wait. Robert has such a full caseload it would have meant waiting for months.

'It was a very quiet wedding with just a lunch afterwards. When we do come to England, Robert says we'll have a huge party and invite everyone.

'I'm enclosing some photographs so that you can see how handsome Robert is and how happy we are.'

In a daze, Sorrel opened the packet and took out half a dozen photographs. Robert Jackson was certainly attractive in a particularly American way. He had close-cut hair, and white teeth gleamed in his tanned face. Alyse, in a pretty, long cream dress, was glowing with happiness. Mrs Goldman smiled proudly as if she had brought about the whole thing on her own.

Sorrel looked again at the photographs of the bride and groom. Their faces, as they gazed at each other, radiated love and happiness. So that was what Alyse wanted. Robert Jackson was very different from Marcus.

Marcus! What would he think? In helping Alyse to regain her health, he had lost her. Did he know what had happened? Would she be the one to tell him?

She turned again to the letter.

'I have written to Marcus. I hope he won't mind about the wedding. He didn't exactly send me here to get married, did he? But he's such a sweet, kind person, I'm sure he'll be happy for me.

'Will you show him the photographs? I haven't sent any to him. And make him see how incredibly happy I am and that it's really because he helped me.

'Robert and I won't have a honeymoon for a while, and we're living with Mrs Goldman until I'm quite better, so you can write to me here.'

Letting the letter drop into her lap, Sorrel sat, unmoving, until it began to get dark outside. She just couldn't take it in. Alyse married! Alyse never coming back to live with her.

She would have liked to discuss it with someone, but who? It was too late to disturb Donna. Perhaps she would go to Penrose and talk to Nicole after work tomorrow.

Realising that she hadn't eaten, she went downstairs and into the kitchen. But as she poked about in the cupboards she realised she had no appetite, and instead poured herself a glass of wine and sat at the kitchen table. Alyse married. It seemed impossible.

She was in such a deep reverie that the sound of the telephone made her jump and spill her wine.

'Sorrel, it's Marcus. Can I come round?' His voice was abrupt.

He must have had a letter too, and wanted to talk about it with her, she supposed. But what could she say to him? She was in a state of shock herself. How could she comfort him?

'Sorrel, are you still there?'

'Yes. Yes, of course you can come round.'

She took another wine glass from the cupboard — Marcus would need something more than coffee — and carried the glasses and the bottle upstairs. She drew the curtains, switched on the electric fire and a table lamp. The room looked cosy. Perhaps that would help if the next hour proved to be as difficult as she feared.

She was still wearing her working clothes but she felt a softer look was called for. Rushing into her bedroom, she flung off her black trousers and took a soft blue and white skirt from the wardrobe. She was just freshening her lipstick when the front door bell rang.

Marcus followed her upstairs and accepted a glass of wine.

'You've heard? That's a bit of a shock, isn't it?' He took a letter with an

American stamp from his pocket and put it on the table next to Sorrel's own letter.

She searched his face for signs of grief or anger, but could find none.

'Are you — upset?' she ventured.

'Upset? No. Surprised, of course. And I feel I ought to be unhappy because she's not coming back, but I'm not. I sent her there to be made better; if she's also acquired a husband, I'm pleased. Why should I be upset?'

'You're very fond of Alyse. I thought a letter with such news would upset you.'

'Yes, I'm very fond of Alyse. Who wouldn't be? But I'm not in love with her. You didn't think that, did you?'

She felt her cheeks flush and looked down at her wine glass.

'Sorrel, you didn't think I was in love with Alyse?' he pressed.

'Sometimes I wondered,' she finally said in a quiet voice.

'And what about you?' he asked after a short silence. 'Were you upset when Carl Schumann left so suddenly? And when you discovered he was married?'

Her head shot up. 'Carl? Why on earth should you think that would upset me? You didn't think I was in love with him?'

The tone of her voice convinced him. He poured them both another glass of wine.

'It seems we were both mistaken,' he said.

He reached into an inside pocket of his jacket and brought out a creased, rather worn envelope.

'This is the letter that really upset me. Do you recognise it?'

Sorrel looked at the envelope and then at him. His deep grey eyes were boring into her. *Her* letter. He had kept her letter all these years.

'I know that what I did was unforgivable,' he went on. 'We'd been so much to each other. Looking back, I can't believe it happened. But I was young and completely under the influence of my father. You remember what he was like?'

Sorrel nodded. Felix Barrington had frightened everyone with his harsh, domineering ways. Pamela had been the only one who could handle him, but even she had never dared cross him.

'I told him I loved you,' said Marcus. 'You never knew that because we never spoke of it again.'

'What — what did he say?'

'There was a terrible row. I can't tell you all of it,' he said with disgust. 'He admitted that he had nothing against you except that you had no money, and he had found a girl who had a fortune. There was no contest.'

'So it all came down to money?'

'To be fair to him,' said Marcus, 'if I hadn't married money, we should have lost the estate. It had been in the family for four hundred years. He saw himself as the custodian. It was all he thought of — that and Pamela.'

'So you were sacrificed.'

'We were sacrificed.' He looked at the envelope sadly. 'This was all I had left of you. But such a bitter letter.' He took her hand. 'Surely you didn't believe I *wanted* to part from you?'

'How could I not believe it? You'd left me. I'd lost you.' She bit her lip to hold back the tears. 'You never replied. I thought the letter meant nothing to you.'

'I couldn't,' he said quietly. 'I tried several times, but the right words wouldn't come. The letter has been with me ever since, but I couldn't reply. I'm sorry.'

There was a pause, then he asked hopefully, 'Is it too late to start again?'

She looked at the handsome face, so close to hers.

'You mean . . . ?'

'I meant it when I said I still love you, darling Sorrel, and I think you might have some feelings for me.'

'Some feelings,' she repeated with a tremulous little laugh. 'You might say that.'

Hope sparked in his eyes. 'You mean — you do love me?'

'I've never stopped loving you,' she

confessed. 'I could never love anyone else.'

He moved from his chair to sit beside her on the couch and enfolded her in his arms.

'My dearest, darling Sorrel, I would do anything to undo the past, but I can't. Perhaps, in time, we can pretend it never happened.'

She put her arms around his neck and his lips found hers. It was a long, sweet kiss.

'We can't pretend it never happened, but we can learn from it,' she murmured. 'We must always be open with each other and discuss problems sensibly. No more bottling things up.'

'Or writing letters,' he teased before he kissed her again.

As they drew apart, his grey eyes were intense on hers.

'Now that we've found each other again, can I ask you the question I should have asked years ago?'

She gazed at him, all her love in her eyes. She knew the question, and there was no doubt what her answer would be.

'My dearest Sorrel — ' His voice was husky with emotion. 'Will you marry me?'

She hesitated for such a long time that a look of fear crept into his eyes. Then she laughed delightedly.

'Of course I will. You have always been and always will be my only love.'

The rest of the evening vanished in a whirl of plans.

'I don't want a big wedding and lots of fuss,' said Sorrel. 'Let's do it quietly, the way Alyse did.'

'Do you want to wait till she comes back?'

'No. When she does, we'll have a huge party. It'll be a wedding party for both of us.'

'If that'll make you happy, I'm satisfied,' said Marcus. 'Now, do you think you could find something to eat? At the risk of sounding unromantic — I'm starving. I came straight from the Barns without stopping to eat.'

She burst into laughter. 'It isn't romantic, but so am I! I've had no dinner either. Let's go and defrost two of Alyse's meals. She can't have had the faintest idea when she made them that they would celebrate an engagement!

★ ★ ★

Sorrel's plans for a quiet wedding came to nothing. They were both too well-known in the town for a simple ceremony, and so many people wanted to help them celebrate.

So, on a crisp winter day, six weeks later, the church by the harbour was filled with flowers and happy wedding guests.

Sorrel's family flew in from Australia, Alyse and Robert came from America, and the rest of the town filled the pews and sang with gusto. A wedding so late in the year was a rare event and everyone wanted to make the most of it.

Sorrel, in a heavy white satin dress

and little velvet cape, looked radiant. She wore a tiny fur hat and carried a fur muff to keep out the cold winds from the sea.

Marcus, handsome in morning dress, beamed proudly. Sorrel had captured the town's most eligible man, but she was popular and everyone was happy for her.

The reception was small and intimate; only family and close friends were invited. But for the evening, they had planned a big celebration party at Pencarrock Barns.

Sorrel had mixed feelings about this. She wanted friends and neighbours to enjoy her wedding, but she longed to be alone with Marcus, to make up for lost time.

She looked round the table. Her parents, whom she hadn't seen for more than a year; Alyse and her new husband; Nicole and Carreg, close, caring friends; all the people she loved best. What a wonderful day this had been! And most wonderful of all, at last she and Marcus were together for all time.

She even tried to smile at Pamela but was rebuffed as her sister-in-law turned her head away. However, Sorrel refused to be upset. Pamela was a problem for the future which, with Marcus's help, she knew she would solve.

She turned and gave her new husband a radiant smile and his surprising response was to smile at her and put a finger to his lips. Then he left the table, collected up her parents, and Alyse and Nicole, and took them to the far end of the room, while she watched in bewilderment.

When they all returned, they each embraced Sorrel and wished her a wonderful honeymoon. Baffled, she looked at Marcus.

'What's going on?'

'You'll see . . . ' was his teasing response. He took her hand, and led her from the room and out to his car.

'I'll drop you at the shop,' he said. 'You have half an hour to change and be ready with your suitcase.'

'But I don't understand . . . '

'All will be revealed,' he teased. He slid his arm round her shoulders and pulled her towards him to kiss her passionately. 'That must do for a while, Mrs Barrington. Now, just do as I say — get changed and be ready to leave in half an hour.'

'But the party . . . '

He smiled tenderly into her eyes. 'Do you really want to go to the party? And do you think I can wait another six hours to have my lovely bride to myself? Your parents will be the hosts, everyone will enjoy themselves and we'll be far away.'

He stopped the car in front of the shop, came round to her side and helped her out, taking care not to mark her dress.

As she reached the door, it opened and Alyse's face looked out.

'There you are, a maid to help you,' smiled Marcus. 'See you in half an hour.'

'How did you get here ahead of us?' asked Sorrel. 'Never mind, it's wonderful to have you to myself. Are you really happy? What a silly question, I only have to look at you. And Robert is a dream.'

Alyse hugged her. 'If you're half as happy as we are, you'll be delirious!' she said. 'But we must hurry. Let me undo your dress.'

With Alyse's help, she was soon out of her lovely wedding outfit and into the slate blue trouser suit with a matching top coat which she had bought for travelling.

'I can't believe this,' she kept repeating. 'I thought we were going tomorrow.'

'Marcus can't wait to get you to himself,' smiled Alyse. 'He's waited a long time.'

'And so have I,' said Sorrel, 'but it was worth the wait.'

★　★　★

305

Marcus drove swiftly along the Romantic Road in Upper Bavaria. Sorrel had been intrigued by the name.

'I believe it's because it passes so many medieval towns,' Marcus explained. 'There's something very romantic about towns preserved as they were hundreds of years ago. They look like illustrations from old story books. Perhaps we'll stop and investigate some on the way back.'

Sorrel was content to look at the snow-covered fields and woods on either side of the road and the huge Alps looming ahead.

Her mind kept returning to the topic they had discussed last night at dinner, and Marcus's solution to her problem.

'I have an empty shop at Pencarrock Barns,' he'd ventured. 'You could have that.'

Sorrel considered. 'It's quite a long way out of town.'

'But you'd have plenty of customers in the season. And perhaps,' he had added meaningfully, 'you wouldn't want to work as much as before. You might have another interest to take up your time.' The loving look he gave her left her in no doubt of his meaning.

A shop at the Barns. The suggestion was certainly worth considering. Marcus was based there and they would be able to see lots more of each other.

He brought her back to the present.

'Look out for a sign on the left that says 'Konigsschlosser'. That means King's Castles. We turn off there.'

They saw the sign soon after this and he swung the car to the left.

Sorrel gave a gasp. 'Look, darling. There it is! At last. I can't believe we're here.'

The castle of Neuschwanstein, towered and turreted, rose above the wooded slope on which it stood. Covered in snow, it glistened and glittered in the sunshine.

To the right of the castle was another, a yellow castle, less dramatic than Neuschwanstein.

'That's Hohenschwangau,' said Marcus. 'The castle of the swan.'

They drove on and parked in the carpark at the foot of the hill.

'There are some horse-drawn carriages to take us up,' said Marcus, 'or we can walk. It'll take about twenty-five minutes,' he warned, 'and it's very steep.'

'We'll walk,' said Sorrel decisively. 'We've been sitting for ages. Come on.'

Setting a brisk pace, she started up the steep hill with its thick woods on either side. The air was crisp and cold but she barely noticed the temperature. She was eager to reach her destination.

At the top of the hill, she stopped suddenly, the view ahead of her taking her breath away. Marcus came up behind and wrapped his arms around her, holding her close as together they looked upwards.

The castle rose above them, higher and higher towards the snow-laden clouds. Sorrel took the little wooden swan from her pocket and held it up in her gloved hand.

'I'm here, Ernst,' she whispered. 'I've

kept my promise.'

Then she turned to Marcus, her beloved, adored Marcus.

'Thank you for making this dream come true.'

He dropped a tender kiss on her lips. 'This is only the beginning for us, my darling. From now on I intend to make sure that *all* our dreams come true . . . '

The End.

We do hope that you have enjoyed reading this large print book.

Did you know that all of our titles are available for purchase?

We publish a wide range of high quality large print books including:
Romances, Mysteries, Classics
General Fiction
Non Fiction and Westerns

Special interest titles available in large print are:
The Little Oxford Dictionary
Music Book, Song Book
Hymn Book, Service Book

Also available from us courtesy of Oxford University Press:
Young Readers' Dictionary
(large print edition)
Young Readers' Thesaurus
(large print edition)

For further information or a free brochure, please contact us at:
Ulverscroft Large Print Books Ltd.,
The Green, Bradgate Road, Anstey,
Leicester, LE7 7FU, England.
Tel: (00 44) **0116 236 4325**
Fax: (00 44) **0116 234 0205**

Other titles in the
Linford Romance Library:

PORTRAIT OF LOVE

Margaret McDonagh

Three generations of the Metcalfe family are settled and successful — professionally and personally. Or are they? An unexpected event sparks a chain reaction, bringing challenges to all the family. Loyalties are questioned, foundations rocked. A secret is exposed, unleashing a journey of discovery, combining past memories, present tensions, the promise of lost love and new hope for the future. Can the family embrace the events overtaking them? When the dust settles, will they emerge stronger and more united?

A BRIDE FOR JASON

Beverley Winter

Ace reporter Jason Edwards wants to marry Carly Smith, but Carly is a career girl and their families have been feuding for years. When she takes a job with Jason's family her aim is to safeguard her livelihood by exposing their unsavoury dealings. But Jason's instincts compel him to question her motives. Will the truth allow him to overcome the obstacles and still make Carly his bride? And when Carly discovers his reasons for doubting her, can she forgive him?

SNAPSHOTS FROM THE PAST

Angela Drake

When young widow Helen meets Ed her future at last seems bright. Her newfound happiness seems complete until a terrifying new shadow falls across her life. Someone is watching her, tracking her movements and sending her chilling photographs through the post — pictures relating to her past. Soon Helen can trust no one, and when her suspicions finally fall on Ed, their relationship is shattered. But who is Helen's tormentor? And will she and Ed ever get together again?

KISS AND TELL

Diney Delancey

When Ginny agreed to take her sister's place as au pair to two children on a skiing holiday in Austria, she wondered what she'd let herself in for. She'd been warned that Gareth Chilton, the children's uncle and guardian, was an arrogant — if good-looking — man, and was soon to experience his supremely overbearing manner! But Gareth's tender loving care for his niece and nephew melted Ginny's heart like snow in summer. And that was when her problems really began . . .